CLASS PETS

Fuzzy Freaks Out

CLASS PETS

#1: Fuzzy's Great Escape

#2: Fuzzy Takes Charge

#3: Fuzzy Freaks Out

#4: Fuzzy Fights Back

CLASS PETS
#3: Fuzzy Freaks Out

Bruce Hale

Scholastic Inc.

If you purchased this book without a cover, you should be aware that this book is stolen property. It was reported as "unsold and destroyed" to the publisher, and neither the author nor the publisher has received any payment for this "stripped book."

Text and illustrations copyright © 2018 by Bruce Hale

This book is being published simultaneously in hardcover by Scholastic Press.

All rights reserved. Published by Scholastic Inc., *Publishers since 1920.* SCHOLASTIC, SCHOLASTIC PRESS, and associated logos are trademarks and/or registered trademarks of Scholastic Inc.

The publisher does not have any control over and does not assume any responsibility for author or third-party websites or their content.

No part of this publication may be reproduced, stored in a retrieval system, or transmitted in any form or by any means, electronic, mechanical, photocopying, recording, or otherwise, without written permission of the publisher. For information regarding permission, write to Scholastic Inc., Attention: Permissions Department, 557 Broadway, New York, NY 10012.

This book is a work of fiction. Names, characters, places, and incidents are either the product of the author's imagination or are used fictitiously, and any resemblance to actual persons, living or dead, business establishments, events, or locales is entirely coincidental.

ISBN 978-1-338-14524-3

10 9 8 7 6 5 4 3 2 1   18 19 20 21 22

Printed in the U.S.A.   40

First printing 2018

Book design by Baily Crawford

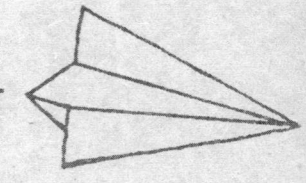

To Blanca Moreno and the cool kids of Doyle Elementary

CONTENTS

Chapter 1: Bad News from a Mouse   1
Chapter 2: Spying on a Specter   12
Chapter 3: Dia de los Monsters   20
Chapter 4: Just Ghost to Show You   29
Chapter 5: If Spooks Could Kill   38
Chapter 6: Miss Tiddy-Bom-Boms   46
Chapter 7: Dr. Prankenstein   53
Chapter 8: A Boom with a View   63
Chapter 9: Scorched Whiskers and Heavy Hearts   70
Chapter 10: Booty on the Bookshelf   78
Chapter 11: A Rat in Spook's Clothing   88
Chapter 12: A Hint of Mint   99
Chapter 13: Pig in a Tutu?   106
Chapter 14: Well and Truly Trapped   117
Chapter 15: Big Ugly's Big Idea   127
Chapter 16: In Arms' Way   136
Chapter 17: Reach for Disguise   146

Chapter 18: Giant Spiders in the Crawl Space … 155
Chapter 19: Chasers Gonna Chase … 163
Chapter 20: Pet Project … 173
Chapter 21: Let the Food Times Roll … 179

CHAPTER 1

Bad News from a Mouse

Something about this spooky-sweet October set Fuzzy the guinea pig's whiskers aquiver. It wasn't just the cool weather. It wasn't just the tang of wood smoke in the air, the Halloween decorations, or even the pumpkin seed snacks that class 5-B's teacher, Miss Wills, always slipped him.

No, this time it was something more. Because this October would be different from the rest.

For as long as he'd been a classroom pet, Fuzzy had always loved the kids' Halloween costumes. On that one magical day each year, his familiar boys and girls transformed into something strange and new. Pirates and princesses, superheroes and skeletons.

Then they always marched off to join the other students in the school-wide costume parade, leaving Fuzzy behind.

Until this year.

This year he would see *all* the students in *all* their outfits. Fuzzy had had the brainstorm this afternoon as Miss Wills was telling the class about life in the thirteen colonies. (He wasn't much of a History Rodent, so that left lots of time to think during social studies.) And now he was scampering through the crawl space on his way to the Class Pets clubhouse, eager to share his idea with his fellow pets.

Fuzzy had been trying for weeks to plan a follow-up to his last adventure, their museum field trip. And now he finally had it.

Purring to himself, he dodged around ducts and struts in the dusty ceiling. Fuzzy just knew the other pets would flip for his idea.

As he approached the ramp leading down into the space above Room 2-B's closet that served as their clubhouse, voices rose to greet him. The other pets were already there—and arguing about something, from the sound of it.

"You can't be a princess," said Cinnabun the rabbit.

"Why not?" squawked Sassafras.

"That's *my* costume," said Cinnabun. "And everyone knows a bunny princess makes much more sense than a parrot princess."

"Parakeet," said the bird.

Fuzzy trotted down the ramp. "Hey, you guys!"

"Sorry, *parakeet*," said the flop-eared rabbit, as if he hadn't spoken. "But parrot, parakeet, or panda, you'll just have to think of something else."

"But—" Sassafras began.

"I've just had the greatest idea!" said Fuzzy.

Batting her big brown eyes at Sassafras, Cinnabun crooned, "Sister, you wouldn't want to cause me costume distress now, would you?"

Sassafras grumbled, but she backed down pretty quickly. The pets generally did. Whether by charm or force of personality, the club's rabbit president usually got her way.

Ever since Cinnabun had hatched the idea of the pets holding their own costume contest, she'd been a one-track bunny. Fuzzy liked costumes as much as the next rodent. But enough was enough.

He sighed. "Doesn't anyone want to hear my plan?"

"I'm all ears, Fuzzy," said Marta the tortoise. She frowned. "Or I would be, if they weren't just holes in my head."

Fuzzy crossed to where she sat, nibbling on a fruit chew. "I finally came up with our next adventure."

"About time," said Igor the green iguana. "I was starting to think you were the club's director of dullness."

Fuzzy tamped down a surge of irritation. Somehow the iguana always managed to get under his skin. "You know how each Halloween the students hold their big costume parade, and we have to stay behind in our classrooms?"

Cinnabun glanced up from admiring her tiara. "Y'all have a costume parade here?" As the newest class pet, she had only been at Leo Gumpus Elementary for a month or so. "Do tell."

"It's amazing." Fuzzy grinned. "All the kids dress up and march around the auditorium to music—at least, that's what Geronimo told me." Geronimo the rat was the club's former president, now retired to a farm.

"*All* the kids in costume?" The rabbit was starry-eyed. "Music and glamour?"

Igor snorted. "But it doesn't matter, 'cause we never get to see it."

Fuzzy raised a finger. "Not this time. This time we'll be right there with them, watching it all."

Marta furrowed her brow. "But how will we sneak out?"

"Leave that to me," said Fuzzy. "I'll work out the details. What I want to know is, is everyone up for it?"

"Count me in," said Sassafras, preening. "It's the biggest show in school."

Cinnabun hopped up onto the presidential podium (actually a fat copy of *The Complete Works of William Shakespeare*). She thumped her gavel on the book.

"Brothers and sisters, we have a motion before us. Brother Fuzzy proposes a Halloween field trip to watch the school's costume parade. All in favor?"

Fuzzy's paws tingled. This was it. Unless something went wildly wrong, he would finally get to witness the magical sight of all those students dressed up in their disguises. His mouth curved in a broad smile.

And then something went wildly wrong.

"Help, help!" squeaked a piercing voice from above.

As Fuzzy turned to look, Mistletoe the mouse came tearing down the ramp. Her eyes were wild, her fur stood on end, and she looked as discombobulated as a ferret on a freeway.

"What's wrong, dear?" asked Marta.

"I just—" Mistletoe began. But she was running so fast, she tripped over her own feet, smacked her head on the ramp, and rolled hibbity-jibbity down to the bottom like a dun-colored mouseball.

Whump!

Fuzzy rushed to his friend's side. "Are you all right?"

"You mean, aside from having a lousy sense of balance?" said Igor, popping a pawful of spicy peas into his mouth.

Fuzzy shot him a dirty look.

Holding her head, Mistletoe sat up, woozy. "Whazza?"

Cinnabun touched her arm. "Steady now, sweet girl. You took an awful spill."

"What was I . . . ?" the mouse mumbled. Suddenly, her eyes bugged out. "A ghost!" she squeaked.

"Where?" Fuzzy flinched, checking behind him.

"Room 4-B." Mistletoe rose to her knees. "There's . . . there's a ghost in 4-B!"

Cinnabun and Sassafras exchanged a glance. Igor rolled his eyes.

"Riiight," said the iguana. "And I'm the grand pooh-bah of Pittsburgh."

The mouse stood, swaying. Fuzzy steadied her.

"But it's true," she said.

"I think I'd know if I was a pooh-bah," said Igor.

"No, the ghost!" panted Mistletoe.

Patting her shoulder, Cinnabun said, "You bonked your head kind of hard there, sugar."

The mouse's eyes went from one pet to another. "No, really, truly, there *is* a ghost. I heard it. I saw it."

Sassafras groomed her wing feathers. "Probably just Mr. Darius, cleaning up."

A deep voice rumbled from the corner. "Nah, I saw the D-Man leaving early today." It was Luther the rosy boa, who had been taking a brief afterschool nap before all the commotion.

"You believe me, don't you, Luther?" asked Mistletoe.

The snake yawned. "I believe that there are more

things in heaven and earth than you can find in a schoolbook, Little Bit. But no, I don't believe in ghosts."

"There you go," said Igor, returning to his snack.

Mistletoe slumped.

"I believe you saw . . . something," said Fuzzy carefully. He knew that his mouse friend was highly excitable, but he'd never known her to lie before.

She clasped his paw. "Thank you. But what are we going to do about it?"

"*Do?*" asked Fuzzy. It had never occurred to him that you did anything about ghosts, other than trying to avoid them.

"Well, yes," said Mistletoe. "We can't just let a phantom hang out in our school."

"Why not?" said Igor. "Leo Gumpus needs more school spirit."

Fuzzy rolled his eyes.

The mouse frowned. "But what if it scares the kids? What if they get . . ." She gulped. "Ghost touched?"

A chill danced across Fuzzy's shoulders. "Ghost touched?"

Cinnabun tried a laugh. It sounded hollow. "Why, fiddlesticks! I don't believe there's any such thing."

Nodding earnestly, Mistletoe said, "I heard if a ghost touches you, you start turning into one yourself."

Igor snorted. "Ridiculous." But doubt flickered in his eyes.

Fuzzy cleared his throat. "Before we get all freaked out about this, maybe someone should go and check out Room 4-B? You know, just to make sure?"

"Um," said Mistletoe.

"Who wants to volunteer?" asked Fuzzy.

He looked at Cinnabun, who looked at Sassafras, who looked at Luther, who looked at Igor, who looked at Mistletoe, who looked at Fuzzy. The mouse would've looked at Marta, but the tortoise had retreated into her shell.

"Really?" said Fuzzy. "You guys don't believe in ghosts, but none of you is willing to go check it out?"

"Busy day," said Igor.

"Important stuff to do," said Sassafras.

Cinnabun smoothed down her chest fur, avoiding Fuzzy's gaze. "All things considered, y'all, this sounds like a job for the Class Pets Club's director of adventure. Who's with me?"

All the animals except Fuzzy raised a paw, front foot, or tail. Fuzzy didn't vote because, as it happened, *he* was the club's director of adventure.

"Majority rules," said the rabbit.

Fuzzy clenched his jaw. *When will I learn not to open my mouth?* he thought.

CHAPTER 2

Spying on a Specter

"Fine," said Fuzzy. His throat felt tighter than a T. rex in a tube top. "I'll go with Mistletoe to check out the ghost."

"*Me?*" the mouse shrank back. "What did I do?"

Fuzzy caught her elbow. "You reported this. You've got to show me where it happened."

"B-b-but—" spluttered Mistletoe.

"Splendid idea," said Cinnabun.

Arching an eyebrow, Fuzzy said, "If it's so splendid, why don't you join us?"

The bunny tittered nervously. "Two's company, three's a crowd. Besides, we already voted." She gave them a little push toward the ramp. "Do let us know what you find."

Fuzzy glanced around at the faces of his fellow pets. Every one of them wore a *better you than me* expression. He blew out a sigh and tugged Mistletoe's arm. "Come on, let's go."

Moving slower than the last minutes before mealtime, she followed him up the ramp and into the dark crawl space.

It smelled of dust, damp wood, and the faint memories of old cafeteria meals. In the best of times, this space above the ceiling gave Fuzzy the creeps. But now, with the subject of ghosts hanging in the air, it seemed twice as spooky. Every creak set his nerves on edge. Every gurgle in the pipes made him twitch.

And then, something touched his shoulder.

Wheek! Fuzzy nearly shot through the roof.

It was only Mistletoe.

"*What?!*" squeaked Fuzzy, his voice higher than a dog whistle. Then he recovered himself and cleared his throat. "Er, what is it?"

"Thanks for believing me," said the mouse. "I know

the other pets think I'm a little, um, flaky. But I'm telling the truth."

"I know," said Fuzzy. Inside his head, two competing voices were saying, *It's probably nothing* and *What if she really* did *see a ghost?*

The closer they came to Room 4-B, the slower their footsteps grew. Finally, the two pets stopped just above the room next door.

"Okay," said Fuzzy in a half whisper, "tell me exactly what happened."

Mistletoe scrunched up her face. "Where should I start?"

"At the beginning."

"Well, I was born in a pet store, sixth in a litter of nine—"

Fuzzy blew out some air. "Not the beginning of your *life*. When you first saw the . . . whatever-it-was."

"Oh." Mistletoe blinked. "Well, I was running late for the meeting, and so I took a shortcut above the fourth-grade classrooms."

"And then?"

The mouse pointed at 4-B. "Just as I was passing over there, I heard a kind of skittering sound below me."

"Skittering?" said Fuzzy.

"Yeah, you know. Sort of a"—she wiggled her fingers to illustrate—"*shh-glck, shh-glck, shh-glck.*"

"Uh-huh." Fuzzy had only the foggiest idea what she was talking about. "Go on."

"It sounded weird," said Mistletoe. "Not like a human. Not like a pet."

"Okay."

The mouse wrung her paws. "So I pulled up a ceiling tile to take a look."

Despite himself, Fuzzy was drawn into her story. "What did you see?"

"At first, nothing. Just a dark room. And then . . ."

Fuzzy leaned forward. "Yes?"

"All of a sudden, this weird light flashed, over by the closet."

Slumping, Fuzzy said, "That's it? You dragged me up here for a light?"

"No, there's more," said Mistletoe. "I called out, 'Who's there?' Then I heard a strange moaning, like *woooo*, and the light flashed all around the room and right into my eyes."

"Huh." It was starting to sound like the mouse had

interrupted a prowler. Scary, maybe. But not ghost scary.

"The moan got louder," said Mistletoe, eyes widening. "And it seemed to come from everywhere."

"So what did you do?"

"I screamed, 'It's a ghost!' and ran away," said the mouse. She shuddered. "I was *terror-fied*. I never saw a phantom before."

Fuzzy scratched his cheek. Most likely, Mistletoe had spotted some human sneaking around after hours and gotten the wrong idea. He felt relieved, but also a tiny bit disappointed.

"Come on," he said. "Let's take a look." When the mouse hung back, Fuzzy added, "Don't worry. I'll protect you."

Together they tiptoed above Room 4-B. Digging his claws under the edge of a ceiling tile, Fuzzy levered it up and set it aside. In the dimness below, he could make out the top of a bookcase.

Fuzzy sat, dangling his legs over the edge.

"Where are you going?" squeaked Mistletoe.

Fuzzy pointed. "It'll be easier to see the whole room from the top of that bookshelf. Do you want to go first?"

Mistletoe backed away from the opening like it was the drooling mouth of a hungry tomcat.

"Okay then," said Fuzzy. "Follow me."

He lowered himself through the gap, dropping lightly onto the bookcase. After a long hesitation, Mistletoe joined him.

"It was down there," she whispered, indicating the supply closet in the corner. "Spookiest thing I ever saw."

They watched and waited. The wind keened at the classroom windows, which revealed a twilight sky beyond. The building creaked. Nothing else stirred.

"Really," said Mistletoe after a few long minutes. "It was right over there."

"Uh-huh," said Fuzzy.

They waited some more.

"And you're sure it wasn't a teacher?" he asked.

"Well . . . pretty sure."

"Or someone from the office?" said Fuzzy. "It's easy to confuse secretaries with ghosts."

The mouse pouted. "I know what I saw. And I positutely didn't smell any humans."

Fuzzy raised his paws in a peace-making gesture. It seemed like the other pets had been right after all.

There was no specter, and the nervous mouse had just made a mistake. Of course, he, Fuzzy, would not have been tricked like that. After all, he was an experienced, savvy guinea pig who—

Shh-glck, shh-glck, shh-glck.

Fuzzy froze. "What was that?"

Mistletoe shrank against his side. "Skittering," she peeped.

Scanning the darkened room, Fuzzy could make out nothing more than the faint shapes of furniture. Not for the first time, he cursed his poor night vision. Where was that sound coming from?

"There!" whispered Mistletoe.

Down in the corner, a bluish light flickered. As Fuzzy watched, it grew steadier, brighter.

"W-who's there?" he called, his voice shaking only the tiniest bit.

The strange noise continued, the light flashed randomly, but no one answered.

Stiff hairs rose on the back of Fuzzy's neck.

"I said, who's there?" he demanded, louder. "Show yourself!"

Ooooooo. A low moan echoed through the deserted room. A solitary piece of construction paper rose from a low table, seemingly lifted by nothing but the light. It floated in the air, as Fuzzy's insides turned to lemon Jell-O.

"Holy haystacks!" he breathed.

Mistletoe seized his arm in a death grip. "It's . . . it's . . ."

"A ghost!" they cried together.

CHAPTER 3

Día de los Monsters

It's one thing to hear a scary story by firelight, surrounded by friends. But it's a whole other thing to meet a spirit in a dark, deserted room.

Fuzzy and Mistletoe ran screaming all the way back to the clubhouse. Huffing and panting, they scurried down the ramp.

The candles were snuffed out. The room lay empty.

"Ahh!" shrieked the mouse. "The ghost got them!"

Fuzzy gripped her shoulders. "C-calm down," he said. "The meeting ended early, that's all."

"What do we do, what do we do?" moaned Mistletoe.

Her fur stood on end like a tiny porcupine, and her eyes bulged, big as beach balls.

Fuzzy scanned the vacant clubhouse. With the lights off and their friends gone, it seemed nearly as spooky as Room 4-B. He knew that was just his imagination talking, but an imagination is a powerful thing.

"We, uh, go back to our rooms," he said.

"But the ghost?"

Fuzzy took a deep breath and let it out, a little shaky still. He licked his dry lips. "We've only seen it in 4-B, right?"

The mouse swallowed. "Right."

"So we'll be safe in our own rooms." *I hope,* he thought.

Mistletoe shivered. "But what do we do about . . ."

"Tomorrow after school, we'll *all* go back there," said Fuzzy. "With the whole club working together, we'll find some way to scare it off. Don't you worry."

"I'm not worried," said Mistletoe, whose heart was hammering so hard, Fuzzy could practically hear it from where he stood. "That's a good plan."

"Thanks," he said. "Just be brave, and we'll be fine."

The mouse nodded. "Oh, I'm brave. I'm totally brave. But Fuzzy?"

"Yeah?"

"Will you walk me back to my room?"

After tossing and turning half the night, Fuzzy at last dropped into a deep sleep. In fact, he slept so deeply, by the time he woke up Miss Wills was already puttering around Room 5-B.

He yawned and stretched. Morning light streamed in through the windows, the teacher hummed a cheerful tune, and yesterday's frights seemed like a distant memory. Leaving his igloo, Fuzzy sniffed around his habitat. All seemed normal.

He turned to see what Miss Wills was doing, and came face-to-face with a skeleton.

Wheek! Fuzzy shot straight into the air. The phantom had struck again!

Miss Wills turned to see Fuzzy cowering in a corner of his cage. "What's wrong, little guy?" she asked. "Got up on the wrong side of bed?"

"The ghost! The ghost!" he cried, even though he knew she couldn't speak guinea pig.

The teacher followed his gaze. "Don't you like our skeleton?"

"*Gah.*"

She chuckled. "Don't worry, it's just paper. See?" Miss Wills flapped an arm of the cutout she'd taped to the nearby cabinet. "We're gearing up for *Día de los Muertos,* the holiday celebrating family members who have passed on."

"Día de los *Monsters,*" muttered Fuzzy, glaring suspiciously at the skeleton.

Miss Wills cocked her head. "If it really bothers you, I can move it."

Fuzzy watched, his heartbeat gradually slowing, as the teacher removed the horrible thing and taped it to the wall near her desk. He loved that about Miss Wills. She might not speak guinea pig, but she knew what a pet needed.

By this time, the fifth graders had begun pouring in. Connor and Heavy-Handed Jake were boasting about the scary movie they planned to see over the weekend. Messy Mackenzie, Malik, and Lily enthused over an upcoming Halloween party, while Spiky Diego and Maya discussed their costumes.

"But everyone's going as a superhero," said Diego. "Instead of being Wonder Woman, why not dress up as something different?"

"Like what?" asked Maya, tossing her skinny braids over one shoulder as she took her seat.

Diego absently ruffled his crest of spiky hair. "Um, a Greek goddess? An astronaut? The Very Hungry Caterpillar?"

She snorted. "I'll think about it."

Miss Wills's class was gripped with Halloween Fever. They couldn't wait to show off their inventive outfits at the school's costume parade. Fuzzy was looking forward to it too. But with all this ghost business, he found that the thought of skeletons and ghouls was making him just a teensy bit nervous.

Halloween felt much more fun when it was just pretend.

Soon, Miss Wills finished putting up her *Día de los Muertos* decorations, the bell rang, and lessons began. All through the day—in between helping kids with math by letting them calculate the monthly cost of caring for a guinea pig, and giving cuddles to those in need—Fuzzy's thoughts kept returning to the ghost.

He had more questions than a twenty-page math test. For instance, why was it haunting their school? And why Room 4-B in particular? How could the pets drive it away and shield the students?

Fuzzy *really* didn't want to return to 4-B. But he tried to swallow his fear. Protecting the kids came first, every time—that was the class pets' solemn oath.

Pacing up and down his cage, Fuzzy pondered. He felt sure he and the others would find answers eventually. But guinea pigs hate to wait.

At long last, the school day was done. The kids and Miss Wills had gone home, and Darius Poole, the janitor, had tidied up the room, slipping Fuzzy a bit of celery as a treat.

When the door closed behind Mr. Darius, Fuzzy sprang into action. He push-push-pushed his plastic platform up against the cage wall, shoving the blocks and ball beside it to form steps. Then, up he scrambled, over the wall and onto the table with an *oof!*

As Fuzzy made his way over the cubbyholes and up the bookcase, he couldn't help thinking of Geronimo the rat. The former Class Pets president had shown the other pets how to escape their cages and encouraged them to form the club. That sly rat would have had lots of ideas on getting rid of ghosts.

Fuzzy shook his head. They'd just have to solve the problem without their former leader. But it sure would help to have someone that clever in their club again.

Making his way through the darkened crawl space, Fuzzy kept a wary eye out for specters, spirits, and creatures of the night. None showed their faces. By the time Fuzzy reached the clubhouse, Mistletoe was giving the other pets a dramatic account of their return trip to Room 4-B.

"And the page just floated through the air?" said Igor, lifting his eyebrows. "All by itself?"

"Abso-tutely," said Mistletoe. She caught sight of Fuzzy coming down the ramp. "Fuzzy, tell them."

"She's right," he said, joining the others. "I saw it with my own eyes."

Igor sent Luther a skeptical look. "Levitating paper? Mysterious lights? Wooo. Spooky-town."

The boa shifted his coils. "Hey, baby. I'm not a superstitious snake, but if the Fuzzmeister says there's something funny going on, there's something funny going on."

"Thanks, Luther," said Fuzzy.

Cinnabun waved her paws. "That's all very well and good, y'all, but what are we fixing to do about it?"

"Do?" said Fuzzy. "I know exactly what we should do."

"What's that?" asked Sassafras.

"Take a field trip to Room 4-B."

CHAPTER 4

Just Ghost to Show You

Everyone had an opinion on that idea. For a long minute there, the overlapping voices made Fuzzy's ears ring.

"No way, no how!"

"It's all a hoax!"

"I don't want to get ghost touched!"

"Does everyone have to go?"

"Ghost-schmost—I need a snack."

Toonk, toonk, toonk! The thumping of a rubber mallet cut through the noise.

"Stop all that carrying on," said Cinnabun, setting down her gavel. "A bunny can't hear herself think." She hopped off the presidential podium and turned to Fuzzy.

"Now, why on earth do you think everyone should visit 4-B?"

Fuzzy ticked off the reasons on his fingers. "First, there's strength in numbers. Second, the ghost threatens all of us and our students. And third . . ."

"Yes?" said the bunny.

"It's an adventure."

Igor snorted. "So is playing hopscotch on the freeway, but you don't see me doing it."

Fuzzy held up his palms. "Hear me out. You guys voted me as the club's director of adventure, right?"

The pets nodded.

"Well, this is a real adventure. The chance to see something supernatural with your own eyes? That doesn't come along every day."

"And that's fine by me," someone muttered.

Fuzzy shook his head. "If we stick together, we'll be okay. Heck, the ghost will probably be scared of us. We might even drive it out just by showing up."

"Hmm." Cinnabun cocked her head, considering. "That's a fair point . . ."

"But what about the ghost touch?" Marta's voice echoed faintly as she drew her head back into her shell.

"I doubt that's really a thing," said Fuzzy. He shot a glance at Mistletoe, and she shrugged in reply. "Come on, guys, what do you say?"

"I don't know . . ." Sassafras said.

"You're not chicken, are you?" asked Fuzzy.

"A parakeet, chicken? Get out of town," said the bird.

The others reluctantly agreed to go. No one wanted to admit to feeling afraid.

Clearing his throat, Fuzzy gestured toward the ramp. "Okay then. What are we waiting for? Let's go check out the spirit."

With shaky legs, he headed up the plank, hoping he wouldn't be alone.

Tentatively at first, the other pets followed him out of the clubhouse and up into the crawl space. Stealthy as spies, they weren't. The pets' feet kicked up dust as they jostled, joked, and *ssh*ed one another. Glancing back at the group, Fuzzy thought that no ghost could withstand such a brave, though disorderly, crew.

Could it?

But the closer they came to Room 4-B, the more the noisemaking and joking faded. Finally, Fuzzy raised his paw, and the group shuffled to a halt.

"We'll climb down onto the bookcase and make our way to the floor from there," Fuzzy whispered. "Since the ghost likes to hang out in the corner by the supply closet, let's not crowd it."

"No problem there," said Marta. "I'm staying as far away as possible."

"Aw, what's wrong?" said Igor, sidling closer. "Are you afraid the ghost might . . . *cootchie-cootchie-coo*?!"

He dug his fingers into her armpits for a vigorous round of tickling. Marta pulled her legs and head in with a shriek.

Cinnabun swatted the iguana. "Brother Igor!" she scolded. "That is no way to treat a fellow pet."

Igor stopped, but Fuzzy noticed he didn't look the least bit sorry. "Geez Louise. Just trying to keep things light."

Marta sniffed. "Not. Funny."

Fuzzy left their rabbit president to smooth things over and went to remove the ceiling tile. A peek through the gap showed a dim classroom. The sun set early these October days.

Something that might have been fake spiderwebs now stretched from the ceiling to various points in the chamber, and paper skeletons hung from the walls. Things in 4-B were looking pretty Halloweeny.

That is to say, spooky.

Fuzzy swallowed. "Just follow my lead," he whispered to the pets, acting as confident as he could manage.

Lowering himself through the hole, Fuzzy dropped down onto the top of the bookcase. After helping Cinnabun and Marta to join him, he then began climbing downward from shelf to shelf. Finally, he stepped onto a handy tabletop and stopped to regroup.

Glancing up, Fuzzy spotted Marta and Mistletoe peering over the edge. Sassafras glided down to join him. The other three pets made their way to his observation post.

When everyone had arrived, Cinnabun whispered, "Whew! Smells like a eucalyptus forest."

"Maybe it's ghost B.O." Igor smirked, elbowing Fuzzy.

"Only if it's a ghost koala," said Luther.

Fuzzy took a whiff and noticed a sharp tang in the air like a thousand unwrapped cough drops. Strange. He hadn't smelled it the day before. Maybe the class was working on some tree-related project?

"Keep your eyes on that corner," said Fuzzy. "That's where the . . . thing showed up last time."

Settling in, they began their vigil. The clock on the wall ticked. Pipes gurgled deep in the building. In the quiet, it felt like the room was holding its breath.

Then a *scritch-scritch-scritch* came from somewhere nearby.

Fuzzy crouched.

Luther tensed.

Cinnabun grabbed Fuzzy's arm. "The ghost?" she hissed.

Looking around, Fuzzy spotted Igor scratching himself with his long fingers. He glared at the iguana.

"What?" said Igor. "I was itchy."

Fuzzy put a finger to his lips, and the pets settled in to wait some more. The minutes stretched like cheese strands from a jumbo pizza. A lonely wind whistled in the window casement.

Luther leaned close. "I'm starting to think that—" he began.

Suddenly, the blue light shone in the corner, flailing madly. A tingle ran along Fuzzy's limbs. He gripped Cinnabun's shoulder. "See?" he whispered.

She nodded, wide-eyed.

A sheaf of papers shot into the air, raining down around the supply table. Someone gasped. When Fuzzy glanced back at his fellow pets, Igor's eyes were as huge as pumpkins and his mouth as puckered as a prune. No smart remarks this time.

"Who's there?" Luther shouted. "Who's doing that?"

No response. The light stopped its wild gyrations.

"Let's make some noise," said Fuzzy.

Everyone began yelling and waving their arms (or in Luther's case, his tail). "Hey! Beat it, ghostie! Yahh!"

Finally, they stopped. The light had winked out. No response from the spirit; all was quiet again. Fuzzy held his breath, waiting.

"Did we scare it off?" asked Mistletoe.

Fuzzy's shoulders slumped. He gave a weak chuckle. "I think—"

In a flash, a glowing white shape zoomed through the air straight at their heads. Fuzzy's blood turned to ice water.

Wiggling whiskers!

"*Aieeee!*" someone screamed. Everyone hit the tabletop.

The phantom soared past, trailing a high, evil cackle and a whiff of eucalyptus.

Fuzzy whirled, every hair on his body standing on end. Where had the creature gone? He heard a pattering of ghostly footsteps. And then, nothing.

Cautiously, Cinnabun looked around. "Where is it?"

Pulling her head out from under her wing, Sassafras scanned the room. "There!" She pointed.

Standing out clearly in the dimness, a line of glowing

tracks trailed along the wall almost to the floor, where they abruptly ended. Strangely, the tracks were tiny shoes.

"Ghostly footprints," said Luther. "It's real, all right. We got ourselves a spook."

In the dimness, something went *thump!*

Fuzzy whirled, expecting more spirit mischief. But all he saw was Igor, flat on his back, eyes closed.

The iguana had fainted dead away.

CHAPTER 5

If Spooks Could Kill

All was pandemonium. In a mad rush, the pets dragged a half-conscious Igor back up into the crawl space. As Fuzzy beat his retreat with the rest, he flashed on something. In the confusion of the spirit's attack, for just an instant he'd been reminded strongly of Geronimo.

Was Fuzzy longing for the rat's cleverness? Why did it feel like that had been *Geronimo's* ghost? But their ex-president was living on a farm somewhere, wasn't he? Unless he'd kicked the bucket and come back to haunt them all . . .

Fuzzy scrubbed his eyes with his fists. Clearly, all this spookiness was messing with his mind.

Sassafras caught up with Igor, who was now walking under his own power. "For someone who doesn't believe in spirits," she said, "you fainted pretty fast."

"I never fainted," said the iguana.

"Everyone saw you, slick," said Luther.

The iguana shook his head vigorously. "I have a low blood sugar condition, that's all. I get woozy when I need a snack."

Sassafras smirked. "Really? Then how about some Ghost Toasties?"

Igor sent her a glare.

"Hold up, y'all," said Cinnabun. "Let's talk."

The group paused at the entrance to their clubhouse.

Fuzzy turned to his fellow pets. "Need any more proof?"

The alarm on their faces was answer enough. The pets looked as shocked as a tapir with its tongue in a light socket.

"I think the words you're looking for are, 'I apologize,'" said Fuzzy.

Cinnabun clasped her paws. "Dear Sister Mistletoe, Brother Fuzzy, I am so, so sorry for doubting you."

"Apology accepted," said the mouse.

Marta voiced the question on everyone's mind. "So, now that we know it's real, what do we do about it?"

The pets traded dismayed glances. No one spoke.

"Um, scare it off?" said Cinnabun at last.

"But ghosts scare *us*," said Sassafras. "How do you scare off a ghost?"

Fuzzy scratched his chin. "I don't know, but tomorrow is Friday."

Mistletoe frowned. "Are ghosts afraid of Fridays?"

"I doubt it," said Fuzzy. "But it's the day we all go home with students. I say let's think about it this weekend and report back on Monday with our ideas."

"All in favor?" asked Cinnabun.

Still a bit shaken, the pets nodded or raised their paws. Since she'd left her gavel in the clubhouse, the bunny thumped her hind paw onto a beam instead. *Toomp toomp toomp.*

"I officially declare this meeting over," she said. "All of y'all put on your thinking caps, and we'll meet up again on Monday."

As the dazed crew split up to head back to their rooms, Cinnabun turned. "Oh, and fellow pets?"

"Yeah?" said Luther.

"Be careful out there."

"No need to tell me twice," said Fuzzy.

The next day, Miss Wills's class seemed normal enough, with the usual lessons, costume discussions, and talk of weekend plans. But the memory of Fuzzy's spooky encounter hung over it all like a shroud. He felt so unsettled, he couldn't even focus on his plans for sneaking out to watch the costume parade.

When Miss Wills had the students write *calavera* poems about those eerie Mexican skeleton people, Fuzzy found himself composing a limerick that began:

> *There once was a ghost in 4-B*
> *Who scared the toot-toot out of me . . .*

Later in their *Día de los Muertos* unit, the kids started assembling their *ofrenda* for someone they knew who had passed on. As Fuzzy learned, the *ofrenda* was a collection of objects that served as a kind of offering. He couldn't help thinking, *Should I create one for Geronimo? If he's haunting our school, would that make him stop?*

By the time the last bell rang, Fuzzy's nerves were as

frayed as a rottweiler's oldest chew toy. He looked forward to two whole days of peace and quiet. Maybe getting away from school for some calm reflection would help him think of a solution—assuming, that is, he ended up with the right family.

That week, Kaylee Chang's high grade on her language arts project had earned her the honor of pet-sitting Fuzzy over the weekend. Kaylee always seemed so polite and friendly in class, Fuzzy felt sure his visit would be a soothing one.

That feeling lasted all the way up until Kaylee carted his pet carrier through her front door.

A burst of wild guitar music, which sounded like someone strangling an angry yak, pummeled Fuzzy's eardrums. He cringed.

"Mom!" bellowed Kaylee. "I'm home!"

The music continued to wail.

"*MOM!*" Kaylee's yell almost drowned out the guitar.

"In here, Boo-Boo!" came a woman's voice from deeper in the house. "The paint's wet!"

The girl lugged Fuzzy's carrier down a hall toward a room with expansive picture windows. The music grew louder and louder as they approached, until it was like they were standing inside a jumbo jet engine. (Or so Fuzzy imagined, never having stood inside one himself.)

When Kaylee and Fuzzy entered the room, so many colors greeted his eye that Fuzzy thought a rainbow had exploded. Spatters of paint covered the floor, the enormous canvases all around, and the overalls of the tiny woman standing at the easel.

The woman turned, and Fuzzy thought she looked just like Kaylee, except for the smile wrinkles and the streak of blue in her jet-black hair.

"Mom, the music!" yelled Kaylee.

Picking up a paint-smeared remote, her mother pushed a button, and the wailing faded to a dull roar.

"Who's your little friend?" Kaylee's mother asked. She had a smear of green on her cheek and a twinkle in her eye.

The girl held up his carrier. "This is Fuzzy, our class pet. Guess what? Since I was the best student this week, I get to pet-sit him all weekend. We're going to have so much fun. We'll hold tea parties, and play dress-up, and watch movies, and . . ."

Fuzzy's eyes goggled. Who was this girl? Kaylee seemed so quiet in class, but here at home, she never stopped talking.

"Congratulations, Boo, I'm so proud of you." Kaylee's mom kissed her daughter on the cheek, transferring the green smear.

". . . eat healthy treats, and play video games, and maybe even dance," the girl continued.

Her mother scrubbed at the paint on Kaylee's cheek with a rag. "That sounds terrific. Why don't you start by introducing Fuzzy to Miss Tiddy-Bom-Boms?"

"Capital idea, Mother," said Kaylee, affecting a British accent. "Perhaps Miss Tiddy will join us for tea and crumpets. Of course, I'll have to put oodles of milk in her tea, and she'll only eat the crumpets if they have fish in them, and . . ."

"Have fun, honey," her mother said, picking up the paintbrush again. "Snacks are in the fridge. I'll be out in a bit."

Kaylee hauled Fuzzy back down the hall into a bright, tidy living room. "Oh, Tiddy!" she called. "Miss Tiddy-Tiddy-Bom-Boms!" Setting down the carrier, she lifted out Fuzzy with eager hands. "She's going to wuv-wuv-wuv you, Mr. Fuzzy. Yes, she is!"

Why did some humans insist on talking to pets as if they were babies? Fuzzy had no idea. But as long as the snuggles and treats kept coming, he was inclined to be a forgiving sort of rodent.

"Oh, Tiiiiddy," Kaylee sang, "where aaaare you?"

As they rounded the corner into the TV room, Fuzzy caught a strong whiff of something that smelled awfully familiar. It wasn't hamster. It wasn't hedgehog . . .

"*There* you are!" cried Kaylee.

She strode right up to an overstuffed armchair, and there, sprawled across the top, was an enormous orange-and-white cat with a smooshed-in nose. Without even consulting Fuzzy, Kaylee held him out to the creature, as if offering a gift. Fuzzy tensed.

The cat opened a pair of headlamp-sized eyes, sniffed, and said, "How sweet. A snack."

CHAPTER 6

Miss Tiddy-Bom-Boms

For a long moment, Fuzzy stared at the cat, and the cat stared right back. Miss Tiddy-Bom-Boms had the better stare. Before long, Fuzzy's legs quivered and his heart thumped against Kaylee's hand like a coffee-crazed drummer.

Tiddy was just joking about the snack thing, right? Fuzzy was too big for a cat to eat—even a whopper of a cat like this one.

Or so he hoped.

"Uh, hi," he said, trying to sound casual. "The name's Fuzzy."

"So?" said the cat. She leaned forward to give him a

thorough sniffing. Unsure what to do, Fuzzy sniffed back.

Miss Tiddy smelled of milk, and attitude, and tuna fish breath. She finished the sniff-down and stared at Fuzzy awhile longer. "Gerbil?" she asked.

"Guinea pig," he said.

"But you're a rodent, right?" The tips of two gleaming white fangs showed when she smiled.

"Uh, yeah." Fuzzy swallowed hard. "A big one."

Miss Tiddy's eyes narrowed to slits. Her tail twitched. "Mmm. I like rodents."

Fuzzy didn't know if she meant as a friend or as an appetizer, so he said nothing.

"I just knew you two would get along," said Kaylee, oblivious of the whole exchange. "Come on, Mr. Fuzzy. Let's go to my room."

With pleasure, thought Fuzzy.

Back into the carrier he went. The girl took him to a cheerful-looking bedroom of yellow walls plastered with posters and the world's largest collection of stuffed animals.

Not for nothing, but Fuzzy wondered what the whole attraction was with stuffed animals. They couldn't move, they couldn't speak. Who would bother with them when the real thing was so much more marvelous?

For the next few hours, Fuzzy's time was taken up with a whirlwind of activities. They enjoyed tea and treats, played video games, snuggled, listened to Kaylee's favorite band, read a book about a gorilla, met each one of the stuffed animals, and did homework. Through it all, Kaylee kept up a steady stream of chatter.

Fuzzy didn't mind it so much—especially the snacks

and snuggles—but all this hustle-bustle did make it hard to concentrate on the ghost problem. Saturday passed in the same hyperactive fashion. Fuzzy was so worn out by Kaylee's constant energy that whenever he wasn't being her playmate, he found himself taking a nap. Several times, Miss Tiddy-Bom-Boms prowled past with a hungry look, but each time, Kaylee sent the cat packing.

By Sunday morning, Fuzzy hadn't had a single productive thought about getting rid of 4-B's ghost. Not one! He worried he was letting down the other pets. Worse, he was letting down the students he'd sworn to protect. Fuzzy pressed his lips together, vowing to work all day long on the problem. No way was he going back to school empty-handed.

But Kaylee had other ideas.

Once more, she invented enough activities to keep a whole troop of Girl Scouts busy for a week. Most weren't so bad, but Fuzzy really could have done without the pink nail polish on his claws. It undermined his macho image.

Finally, after dinner, Kaylee and her younger brother, Jason, flopped onto the couch to watch TV. She placed Fuzzy's cage on a table beside them.

Ignoring the cartoon about wacky talking animals,

Fuzzy settled in to gnaw on a wooden block and think. He hoped the other pets were having better luck. So far, his biggest accomplishment had been avoiding being eaten by Miss Tiddy-Bom-Boms.

Gazing into space, he recalled the creepy ghost of 4-B zooming straight at them. It made him shiver. *Think, Fuzzy,* he told himself. Spirits must have some kind of weakness, aside from not having a body.

What did phantoms hate, he wondered? *And how could you drive out something you couldn't even touch?*

As he mused, a new animated show came on, something about a bunch of teens and a big goofy dog that solved mysteries together. Fuzzy shook his head. The stuff these humans watched!

But his ears really pricked up when the characters on-screen started talking about ghosts. Fuzzy pressed against the cage bars to watch. He gasped when the friends and their dog were ambushed by a glowing spirit that swooped over their heads and sent them screaming.

Just like Fuzzy and his fellow pets!

His eyes widened. How would the dog and his friends defeat the ghost?

"Kaylee! Jason! Time for bed," their mother called.

No, thought Fuzzy. *Not now.*

"Aw, five more minutes, Mom," Kaylee pleaded. "It's just getting to the good part."

Fuzzy could not have agreed more. He gaped as the gang on-screen collected materials for a mystic ceremony to drive away the ghost. They brought a mirror and candles, garlic cloves and other necessities, then they settled down in the dark house to wait. And just when the clock struck midnight . . .

Whump! Something swatted Fuzzy on the back.

Wheek! He jumped straight up in the air. Had the ghost of 4-B followed him to Kaylee's?

Whump, thump! Again, the unseen presence struck him. Fuzzy twisted desperately, and saw Miss Tiddy pulling back her paw for another strike.

Wheek, wheek! he cried. Fuzzy ducked under the cat's swing.

"Tiddy, no!" yelled Kaylee. "Bad kitty!" The girl pivoted on the couch and scooped up the cat in her arms. "That's not how we treat our guests."

The massive cat pasted an innocent expression onto her mug. "It's all a misunderstanding," she meowed, softly as a summer sunrise.

"Yeah, right," said Fuzzy.

"Honestly, we were just playing," the cat protested. Since Kaylee clearly didn't speak cat, and Fuzzy didn't believe a word of it, the creature's pleas were wasted. The girl carried Miss Tiddy to the kitchen and shut the door on her.

Returning to the couch, Kaylee gently picked up Fuzzy for a cuddle. "So, so sorry. I should have stopped her before she got to you."

Fuzzy turned his attention to the screen, but just then, Mrs. Chang entered the room, grabbed the remote, and clicked off the TV.

"Aw, *Mommm*," chorused Kaylee and her brother.

"Time for bed, you two. Now brush your teeth and get ready."

Wiggling whiskers! Fuzzy clenched his jaw. Now he'd never find out whether the ghost-banishing ceremony worked.

Ten minutes later, as Kaylee set his cage beside her bed and turned off the light, Fuzzy reflected, *At least I've got the start of an idea.*

He only hoped it would be enough. Because with a ghost, he suspected, you didn't get second chances.

CHAPTER 7

Dr. Prankenstein

Monday morning found Fuzzy feeling a bit more chipper. Maybe it was from being back in his own home, or maybe it was due to the fresh pine shavings Miss Wills had laid down. Fuzzy liked to think it was because he had the beginnings of a plan.

That morning, the upcoming Halloween Costume Parade was all the students could talk about. True, one or two of the girls seemed less than enthusiastic about "dressing up like little kids," but the rest of the class couldn't wait.

"My *calavera* costume will blow you away," boasted Amir.

"I seriously doubt it," said Maya, "since I'm going as Storm."

Even Heavy-Handed Jake was looking forward to dressing up. His costume? A snow globe of Hawaii.

Fuzzy beamed. He couldn't wait to see his students and the other classes at Leo Gumpus parade through the multipurpose room, transformed into strange and wonderful things. No longer would the pets be left out of the fun. This time they'd be a part of it all.

Assuming, that is, they could dispose of that troublesome ghost first.

After school, Fuzzy waited impatiently for Mr. Darius to come clean up so he could join his fellow pets in the clubhouse. But this time, the janitor wasn't alone.

A sturdy woman in blue coveralls entered behind him. As short as Mr. Darius was tall, the woman followed in his footsteps, squinting suspiciously around the room.

"Such a mess," she sniffed. "Papers pinned to the wall, projects everywhere . . ."

Mr. Darius smiled. "It's called creativity, Rhonda."

"Well, I wouldn't allow it."

"That's the teacher's domain," he said, pushing his

broom along. "Our job is to sweep the floors, mop up spills, and empty the trash, that's all."

Rhonda the Squinty gasped when she spotted Fuzzy. "Look! They're keeping some sort of rat. I *hate* rats." Her face curdled like a bowl of milk left in the summer sun.

Fuzzy chuffed and drew himself up. "I'm a guinea pig!"

Shaking his head, Mr. Darius said, "That's no rat. That's Fuzzy, their class pet. Fuzzy, this is Mrs. Drone, my new assistant."

The squinty woman gave him a funny look. "You talk to animals?"

"Fuzzy's my buddy," said the janitor. "It'd be rude not to include him."

Rolling her eyes, Mrs. Drone muttered, "I still think it looks like a rat."

"Why don't you empty the trash cans into our bin?" said Mr. Darius. He watched her go, then swept the dirt into a dustpan.

"What's with her?" asked Fuzzy, even though he knew the man couldn't understand.

Mr. Darius fished a piece of cucumber from his overalls pocket and slipped it through the cage bars.

"She'll get the hang of it eventually," he said. "Everyone thinks it's a piece of cake being a janitor. But it's not. Really, we're problem solvers."

"Sure," said Fuzzy, just to keep up his end of the conversation.

"For example, someone's been making a mess in the fourth-grade classrooms after hours. Things have gone missing."

Fuzzy stopped chewing his treat.

"I don't know if it's the staff, the kids, or something else altogether," said the janitor, "but see what I mean? I've got to solve that problem."

Fuzzy swallowed his mouthful with difficulty. He knew what was making those messes, and it wasn't teachers or kids.

The tall man chuckled. "Hey, you and your friends haven't been partying after hours, have you?" Noticing Fuzzy's wide-eyed look, Mr. Darius said, "Easy buddy, just kidding."

Fuzzy assumed the phantom was responsible for the mess. But how could he tell Mr. Darius? Not for the first time, he wished that the man spoke guinea pig.

As Mr. Darius finished sweeping the floor and Mrs. Drone emptied the trash, Fuzzy reflected. Maybe it was just as well that the janitor didn't know. After all, he doubted that Mr. Darius's cleaning supplies included a handy bottle of Ghost-B-Gone.

"Are we done yet?" asked Mrs. Drone. "That rodent is watching me with a hungry look."

As if, thought Fuzzy. He wouldn't eat an assistant janitor if his life depended on it.

"All done," said Mr. Darius. With a cheery, "Later, little buddy!" he ushered Mrs. Drone out, closing the door behind him.

Quick as he could, Fuzzy pushed together his blocks, ball, and platform, making his escape. As he scampered across the room and up the bookshelf, he said a silent thank-you that so far none of the humans knew that the class pets could leave their habitats at will.

That would make things as awkward as a hippo on a high wire. The pets were much better off if the humans didn't understand how clever they really were.

Fuzzy scurried through the crawl space, keeping a watchful eye out for stray ghosts. He couldn't wait to share his discovery with the other pets. As he approached the clubhouse entrance, the chatter of voices rose from below. Some of the others had already arrived.

Fuzzy trotted down the ramp, full of his news. Below, he spotted Mistletoe, Cinnabun, and Sassafras, deep in conversation. Seeing Fuzzy, the mouse stiffened and raised a paw. "Look—"

"Hey, you guys," Fuzzy interrupted. "You'll never guess what I saw on—"

Just as he neared the bottom, a dark shape sprung from the shadows beneath the ramp, right into his path.

Suffering mange mites!

"*Rrruagh!*" cried the short, green werewolf.

"Yikes!" yelped Fuzzy, his fur standing on end. He was so startled, he jumped straight up, landed on his butt, and slid the rest of the way down, landing at the creature's feet.

"Don't eat me!" he squeaked, holding up his paws. "I don't taste good."

The werewolf laughed so hard, it jackknifed at the waist, revealing the top of a reptile head behind the mask.

"Now, Brother Igor," Cinnabun chided. "That's plain cruel."

"But funny," gasped the iguana, removing his mask. "Ha! Gets better every time."

Fuzzy scowled. "This is no time for jokes," he rumbled.

Wiping away tears of laughter, Igor said, "Oh, I disagree. With everyone getting so serious, it's the perfect time for jokes."

Mistletoe helped Fuzzy rise. "Don't worry, he scared me too." She stuck her tongue out at Igor. "Majorly unfunny."

Now that the fright was past, Fuzzy felt his heartbeat returning to something like normal. "Where did he even find a werewolf mask that small anyway?"

Slithering down the ramp, Luther said, "You can thank Mr. Mooney's art class for that. They got some wild *sss*tuff in there, baby."

"Maybe next time I'll be a zombie panda," said Igor, waggling his mask.

Cinnabun ignored him. "What were you saying, Brother Fuzzy?" she asked. "Before you were so rudely interrupted."

As Marta the tortoise trudged down the plank to join the group, Fuzzy filled them in on his inspiration from the TV show.

Marta frowned. "So these teens held some kind of ritual to scare away the ghost?"

Fuzzy nodded. "I guess ceremonies affect spirits. Miss Wills said that in Mexico, humans make offerings to keep ghosts happy. So maybe a different kind of ceremony would drive them away?"

"Did it work on the TV show?" asked Mistletoe.

Fuzzy shrugged, embarrassed. "I, um, don't know. Kaylee's mom turned off the TV."

"Great," said Igor. "Perfect. We're supposed to put ourselves in mortal danger *again*, and you don't even know if this ritual *works*?"

Fuzzy looked down at his toes.

"Did you have a better idea, Brother Igor?" asked Cinnabun.

The iguana shifted his weight. "Well, no, but . . ."

"Did any of y'all?" asked their bunny president.

The other pets shook their heads or studied the floor.

"Well then," said Cinnabun. "I think we should give Brother Fuzzy's plan a try."

Fuzzy sent her a grateful look.

Igor snorted. "Fine. But don't say I didn't warn you."

Clapping her paws together, Cinnabun said, "It's settled, then. In ten minutes, we'll head out to collect everything we need for our little ol' ceremony, then we'll meet up above Room 4-B."

"Why ten minutes?" said Sassafras. "Why not now?"

Cinnabun smoothed down her chest fur. "Because first there's a serious matter to discuss."

"More serious than phantoms?" asked Marta.

The bunny nodded. "Our costume contest."

Fuzzy threw up his paws. "Really? I can't believe you're thinking about that at a time like this."

"Don't you get it, Brother Fuzzy?" said Cinnabun. "If we let all this spookiness affect our plans, the ghost wins." She turned to the other pets. "Do y'all want the ghost to win?"

"No way," said Mistletoe.

"Not me," said Sassafras. The others shook their heads.

Fuzzy rolled his eyes, but he didn't argue. He knew a hopeless cause when he saw one.

"All righty then," said the bunny. "First question: Would I be cuter as an elf princess or a unicorn princess? Let's discuss."

Fuzzy smacked his forehead with his paw. It was going to be a long ten minutes.

CHAPTER 8

A Boom with a View

An hour later, as the sun dipped behind the trees and shadows stretched like skeleton fingers, the pets gathered in the crawl space with their finds.

Fuzzy scanned the circle of faces. "Is everybody ready?"

"Hot to—*mmf*—trot and good to go," Luther mumbled around the garlic clove he held in his mouth. Mistletoe flashed a thumbs-up and a nervous smile.

"You know how *I* feel," said Igor.

"True," said Sassafras. "But nobody cares." He sneered in reply.

"So here's the plan," said Fuzzy. "First, we form a chain and pass everything down into the classroom. Then, when everyone's safely inside, we set up our stuff and perform the ceremony."

Mistletoe's eyes rounded into twin moons of terror as a thought struck her. "But what if the you-know-what appears?"

"Keep your head, stay calm—" Fuzzy began.

"And fly like the wind!" squawked Sassafras.

Although Fuzzy's stomach felt full of butterflies, he tried to keep his expression confident. "Just don't freak out, and we'll be fine."

Mistletoe didn't look terribly reassured.

The pets lined up like a bucket brigade, passing the candles, mirror, garlic, and other items down to Fuzzy. He, Luther, and Cinnabun set the candles in a circle. Working together, they lit them with a pocket lighter borrowed from Mr. Chopra's room.

The other pets stood back to watch.

"What's next?" asked Cinnabun.

Fuzzy tried to recall the TV show. "Um, next we pour a circle of salt around the candles for extra protection." He glanced about. "Where's the salt?"

With a wince, Mistletoe said, "I couldn't find any. But I did bring some white powdery stuff I found in Mrs. Puka's desk. That should work."

Fuzzy scanned the label on the canister. "Did you read this?"

"No, why?"

"It's baby powder."

Mistletoe's nose crinkled. "Eew! What kind of monster would crush babies into powder? That's disgusting!"

"I believe it's *for* babies, not *from* babies," said Marta gently.

"Oh." The mouse blinked. "Never mind."

Hefting the unwieldy canister, she and Fuzzy sprinkled the powder in a circle. They managed to get almost as much on themselves as they did on the floor tiles.

"Now we prop up the mirror over here," said Fuzzy, "so if the ghost sees itself, it'll get scared away."

"And I'll put the garlic next to it," said Luther. "Just in case this spirit is some kind of vampire."

"Vampire?" Sassafras gulped.

"Better safe than bitten," said the snake.

Cinnabun nudged a small bundle of straw. "And what's this for?"

"Um, it's supposed to be sage." Fuzzy lifted his eyebrows. "Igor?"

Shrugging, the iguana said, "Couldn't find any sage in the kitchen, but their brooms had straw. Sticks are sticks, right?"

"You have no idea what sage looks like, do you?" asked Marta kindly.

"Do *you*?" said Igor.

"It'll be fine," said Fuzzy. Lifting the straw and offering one end to Cinnabun, he asked the bunny, "Light me?"

"You're sure this will be all right?" she asked.

"Sure I'm sure," said Fuzzy.

Mistletoe nodded. "They did it on TV, right? What could possibly go wrong?"

"At least five things I can think of," said Igor. "And I'm not a very creative reptile."

Marta's brow wrinkled as Cinnabun retrieved the lighter. "And what's the burning straw supposed to do, dear?" she asked.

"Um . . ." Fuzzy struggled to recall the details from the TV show. "The, uh, ghosts don't like the smoke?"

Mistletoe nodded wisely. "Confuses them, I bet. They don't know where the smoke leaves off and they begin."

"Okay now," said Fuzzy. "While I'm smoking the place up, the rest of you should be chanting something."

"What, like *ooga booga booga*?" said Igor.

"No," said Fuzzy tartly. "Something that encourages the spirit to leave."

"Ooh," said Cinnabun. "I've got the perfect chant. How about: *Ghost, ghost, go away; we don't want you here today?*"

"Works for me," said Fuzzy.

The bunny flicked the lighter, and the straw caught with a *crackle*. As the flame leaped high, she led the others in chanting, *"Ghost, ghost, go away; we don't want you here today!"*

Popping merrily, the fire spread. Fuzzy tried to blow it out like a birthday candle, but the flames only swelled. Suddenly, his paw felt warm.

"Someone, help!" He huffed and puffed some more.

Mistletoe, Cinnabun, and Sassafras blew on the burning straw. But instead of extinguishing, the fire doubled in size, gobbling up the straw like jungle ants munching a cow carcass.

"Yikes!" cried Fuzzy. He tried waving the bundle about, but it burned even faster. "Quick, get water!"

Luther streaked off. The other pets backed away.

"Don't worry!" squawked Sassafras. "I've got it." The parakeet fanned her wings, which only fed the flame.

"Not helping," Fuzzy growled through clenched teeth. The fire was only inches from his fingers; its heat beat against his paw like a tiny sun. Desperate, he scanned the room for somewhere to put his torch that wouldn't burn the place down.

"Drop it!" cried Igor.

"Douse it!" squeaked Mistletoe.

"*The ghost!*" yelled Cinnabun, pointing toward the corner with a shaky paw. "Everyone: *G-ghost, ghost, g-go away . . .*" She tried restarting the chant, but the other pets were too terrified to join in.

The white, billowing figure loomed in the corner.

Igor's eyes rolled up into his head, and he fainted. Again.

Fuzzy staggered back.

Toom!

He tripped over something and fell heavily, squishing an uncomfortable plastic container.

Foom!

A cloud of white dust billowed around him. The burning straw flew from his paw into the air.

And before Fuzzy could even blink . . .

Ka-BOOM!

A blinding flash, and the *whoomp* of an explosion drowned out everything else.

The stillness that followed was broken only by the *ssshhh* of a snake spitting water.

CHAPTER 9

Scorched Whiskers and Heavy Hearts

The only upside of nearly blowing up a classroom is that it startles not just pets, but anyone and anything nearby. Including ghosts. Sometime shortly after the blast, the phantom just disappeared.

Not that Fuzzy noticed. So dazed was he that the entire scene, including the pets' rapid retreat from 4-B, was basically a blur. Not until the others had dragged him back to the safety of their clubhouse did he hear the whole story.

"It was awe-*mazing!*" squeaked Mistletoe, eyes wide. "When you knocked over the baby powder, a big old cloud of it went *boof!* And then it *exploded*! I never knew clouds could explode."

Marta sniffed. "And humans powder their young with that stuff? I call that irresponsible."

Fuzzy sat up on his pillow. "Did we burn down 4-B?"

"It's barely scorched," said Cinnabun, "thanks to Brother Luther."

The boa ducked his head. "Aw, it wasn't nothing, Missy Mis*sss*."

"*Nothing?*" scoffed Mistletoe, waving her arms about. "He climbed all the way up to the sink, got a great golliping mouthful of water, and slithered back just in time to spray it on the straw."

"Put the flames right out," Sassafras confirmed.

Mistletoe's eyes shone. "Luther's a genuine hero!" She held up a paw in front of him. "High five!"

The snake arched a brow and glanced at his own sleek, armless body. When the mouse stammered in embarrassment, Luther said, "I'll settle for a fist bump."

He tapped his head against Mistletoe's knuckles.

"But what about the ghost?" asked Fuzzy.

The other pets exchanged uneasy glances. "We don't know," said Marta. "It vanished right after the boom."

"Is it gone for good?" said Fuzzy.

"Most likely it's *sss*till there," said Luther. "I heard a creepy moan as we were leaving."

"Probably Igor," said Sassafras.

The iguana stuck out his tongue at her.

Fuzzy scanned his friends' faces. "Did anyone stay to check?"

The pets shook their heads.

With a dainty shrug, Cinnabun said, "All of us lit out of that classroom faster than a hot knife through butter. I do hate to leave a mess for Mr. Darius, but I'm not fixing to go back there while that ghost might still be around. Any volunteers for cleanup crew?"

The others shook their heads.

It looked like their plan had failed. Again.

Fuzzy tugged his whiskers, which felt slightly singed. "Sorry, you guys. Those TV people seemed so confident, I was sure it would work."

"If only we'd used sage instead of straw . . ." Sassafras began.

"Or salt instead of baby powder," said Igor.

"And if wishes were lunches, we'd all be fat and sassy," said Cinnabun. "Look, everyone tried, but I expect we've still got ourselves a ghost."

Fuzzy slumped. He'd let his friends down again. Heck, he'd let the students down, and now he was fresh out of ideas. Some adventure director he'd turned out to be. Fuzzy dropped his chin onto his paws.

Nobody spoke. The pets avoided one another's eyes.

"So that's it?" said Mistletoe. "We just leave it there? We leave all those kids at risk?"

Fuzzy opened his mouth to say *yes*, but instead found himself saying, "No."

"No?" said Marta.

"That's, uh, not who we are," said Fuzzy, his brain catching up to his mouth. "That's not what a class pet does. And if it takes us a month to scare off that ghost, then it takes us a month. We don't just roll over and give up."

"Yeah, baby," said Luther. "When the going get*sss* weird, the weird get going."

Fuzzy stood. "That's right. Maybe I came up with one idea that didn't work, but I bet someone can come up with a better idea that does."

"Even me?" asked Mistletoe.

"Even you, baby," said Luther.

Fuzzy paced. "The problem is, it's like we're working blindfolded. We don't know that much about phantoms."

"Don't wanna know," mumbled Igor, staring at the floor. His two encounters with the spirit had left him a lot more shaky and a lot less snarky.

"If only we could consult something," said Fuzzy. "A ghost expert, maybe, or a supernatural library."

Luther snorted. "I doubt the school library is up to the task."

"Ooh!" Sassafras's eyes grew round as cantaloupes and a smile curved her beak. "But I know a library that is."

"Which one?" asked Fuzzy.

"It's called . . . the Internet!" The bird spread her feathers dramatically.

Cinnabun's forehead crinkled. "That doohickey on the computer?" Most of the pets had heard of the Internet, but none of them except Sassafras had ever dared to try using a computer.

"Isn't it just a series of tubes?" Marta asked.

The parakeet strutted a little. "It's a lot more than that, ladies and germs. It's like the world's smartest human—you can ask it anything."

"Like why you're so obnoxious?" said Igor.

"Or why iguana brains are so tiny," said Sassafras. "All I have to do is fly over to a computer, type in my question, and it'll tell us how to get rid of that ghost."

"Really?" said Mistletoe.

"Really, truly," said Sassafras.

Fuzzy grinned. "Then I have just one question for you."

"Yeah?"

"What are we waiting for?"

Strangely enough, Sassafras was right. Researching how to trap a ghost took far less time than assembling the materials for the trap. Full night had fallen when at last Fuzzy, Sassafras, Cinnabun, Mistletoe, and Luther accomplished their goal. (Marta and Igor stayed behind.) And although nobody wanted to visit the haunted classroom in the dark, they dredged up their courage and set off.

Creeping carefully through the crawl space with the glass jar and its contents—the honey, the candle, and the crystal attached to a battery—the group paused just above Room 4-B.

"Do you think it's asleep?" whispered Mistletoe.

"I don't believe spirit*sss* need to nap," said Luther. "No bodies, you know?"

They discussed that for a moment or two, as the snake settled the candle stub into the gooey honey that covered the jar's bottom. Fuzzy lit the candle, and Cinnabun added the other items.

All was ready.

"I vote we leave the ghost trap on top of the bookshelf," said Fuzzy. "That way, the humans won't mess with it."

"Also, we won't have to go all the way into the room," added Sassafras.

"That too," he agreed.

"All in favor?" whispered Cinnabun.

"Aye," everyone murmured.

"Then that's what we'll do," said their bunny president.

Luther looped his coils around the jar, and the other pets gently lowered him onto the bookcase.

"All clear?" asked Fuzzy.

"*Ssso* far, *ssso* good," hissed the boa. He settled the ghost trap in position and slithered back up into the crawl space. The others quickly replaced the ceiling tile.

"What now?" asked Mistletoe.

"Now," said Fuzzy, "we wait."

He only hoped they wouldn't have to wait too long. If the pets didn't catch the phantom soon, this Halloween would be a much scarier one than anybody in 4-B could have bargained for.

CHAPTER 10

Booty on the Bookshelf

All through class the next day, Fuzzy couldn't focus. He paced around his habitat—up and down, back and forth. Questions buzzed about his head like fruit flies over a ripe mango. Would the trap work? Had they caught the ghost last night? Could their problem really be over that quickly and simply?

He was dying to know the answers.

After lunch, when several of the girls wanted to bring him out of the cage for a cuddle, Fuzzy was far too wiggly to hold still. Natalia and Messy Mackenzie said, "Ooh, that tickles!" when he writhed in their grip. But when he twisted in Nervous Lily's hands, she tensed up, squealed, and tossed him into the air.

Suffering mange mites!

Fuzzy's eyes popped. It was a long way down to the ground, and guinea pigs aren't known for their flying abilities.

Luckily, Lily had been standing near the beanbag reading chair. After a brief but hair-raising free fall, Fuzzy landed with a *whump!* He checked himself over carefully. Dizzy but unharmed. Feeling rather like the first guinea pig astronaut, Fuzzy vowed to settle down and avoid further spaceflights.

But it was still hard to wait.

Finally, after the school day ended and Mr. Darius and Mrs. Drone had tidied up, Fuzzy could wait no longer. Scrambling out of his cage, he was soon following his familiar route into the crawl space. He knew he should probably wait for the others before checking the trap in Room 4-B, but he just couldn't bear it another minute.

When Fuzzy pushed aside the ceiling tile and gazed down into the darkened classroom, his eyes played tricks. Was that a faint ghostly glow below him, or just dim light reflecting off the jar?

Grasping the ceiling frame's edge, he leaned lower and lower. But he still couldn't tell. Had they caught a ghost or not? Fuzzy stretched to his absolute limit and widened his eyes, peering for all he was worth.

Nothing.

Not for the first time, Fuzzy wished that guinea pigs had better night vision. He went to pull himself back up. But just then, dust tickled his nose. It wiggled, it twitched, and then . . .

"Ahhh-*choo*!" he sneezed.

Fuzzy lost his grip.

Wiggling whiskers!

With a lurch that made his stomach somersault, Fuzzy plummeted straight down into Room 4-B.

Foomp!

He landed heavily on something sticky and hard. Righting himself, Fuzzy felt cold walls curving around him. Thick honey coated his fur.

"Oh no!"

He was stuck inside the jar.

The ghost trap had become a guinea pig trap.

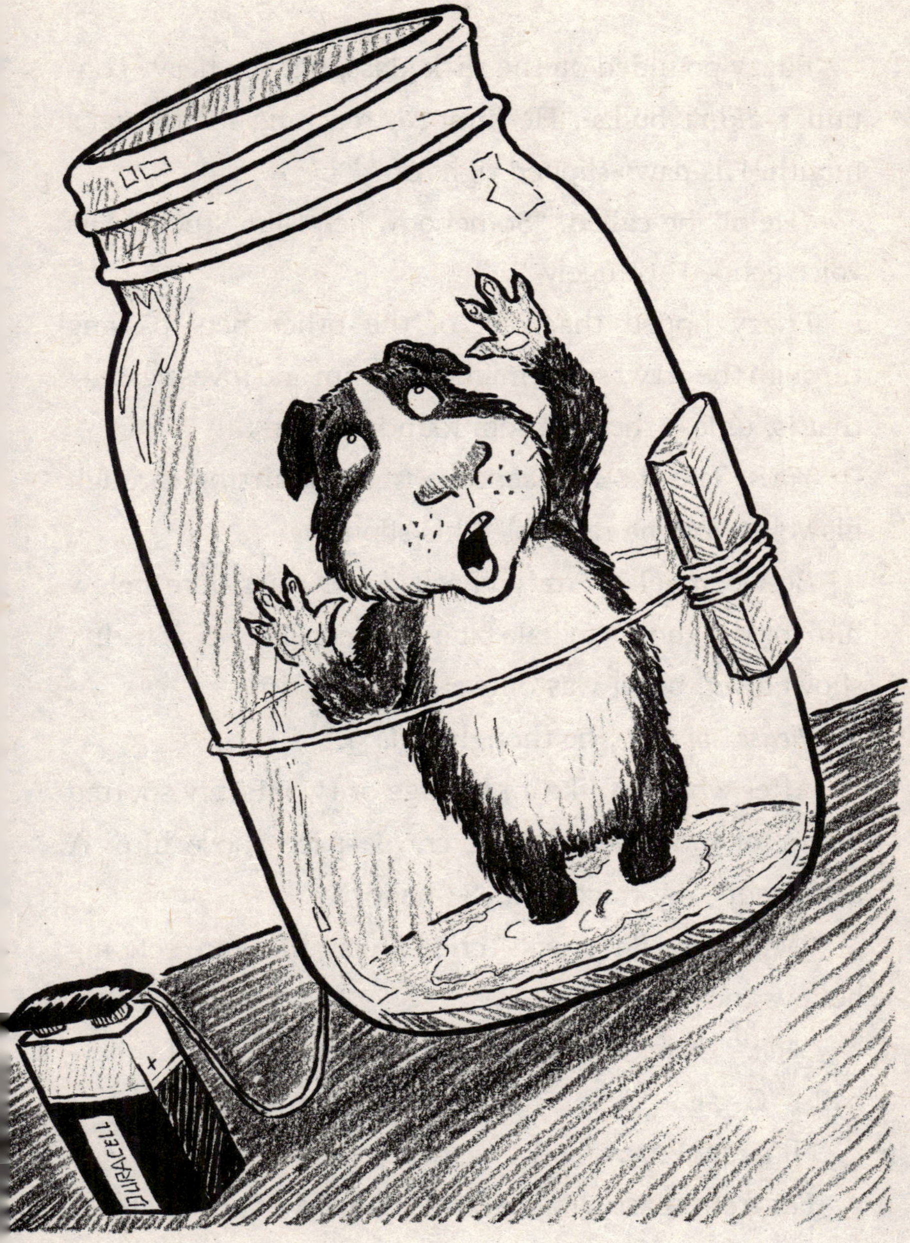
DURACELL

Fuzzy pounded on the slick glass, but the heavy container didn't budge. He jumped, reaching for the jar's mouth. His paws slipped right off.

"Help!" he called. "Somebody, help! I'm stuck!" His voice echoed strangely.

Fuzzy hoped that one of the other pets passing through the crawl space might hear him and investigate—that is, unless the phantom found him first.

Yikes. The thought sent ice water squirting through his veins, and he redoubled his shouting.

Between yells, Fuzzy checked the classroom below him for the ghost's telltale blue glimmer. The spirit hadn't showed yet, but it was only a matter of time.

Please, someone, he thought. *Hurry.*

After what felt like an Ice Age or two, Fuzzy spotted a blur of movement in the crawl space above him. A timid, squeaky voice said, "H-hello?"

"Mistletoe, I'm stuck!" cried Fuzzy, his voice echoing hollow and haunted.

"Aah!" shrieked the mouse, her eyes the size of volleyballs. "G-g-g . . ."

"It's me, Fuzzy!"

Far from reassuring her, this had the opposite effect.

"G-g-guzzy is a fhost!" she cried, leaping straight up.

"No, I'm not. I'm—" He held out his paws to her, which only startled Mistletoe more.

"Melp, melp, a toast!" she yelped. "Gelp, gelp, a host! Relp, relp, a roast! *Aaaah!*" And with that, the mouse streaked away screaming.

"Mistletoe? *Mistletoe!*"

Silence. His friend had gone.

And no matter how he called, she didn't reappear.

Plopping down in the puddle of honey, Fuzzy yanked his whiskers in frustration. Now what? If the other pets believed Room 4-B had *two* spirits, they might never come back.

True, he could eat the honey they'd left in the jar to snare the ghost, but honey wasn't fresh parsley. Not by a long shot.

Fuzzy cast about for an escape plan, and that's when he saw it—

Down below, the bluish glow!

The ghost was back, and Fuzzy had nowhere to run. His limbs tingled with fright. Again and again, Fuzzy slammed up against the side of the jar, trying to tip it over.

No luck.

The white, blobby shape of the spirit floated out of the corner, drifting toward him. Scarier than a weekend at a coyote convention, it drew closer, ever closer.

Fuzzy backed up against the cold glass and froze, transfixed by the sight. Pausing briefly in the middle of the room to moan a creepy *Ooohhh*, it floated onward, making straight for the jar.

Fuzzy's teeth chattered.

The ghost had no mouth, only two holes as dark as graves for eyes. Its unearthly form billowed as if in a supernatural breeze.

A high cackle sent chills spilling down Fuzzy's spine. And then, it spoke.

"Foolish creature!" the spirit keened in a high, eerie voice. "This is *my* domain! Go, or you will regret it."

"I—I can't leave," said Fuzzy. "I'm t-trapped."

"*Eee-ha-ha-ha-ha!*" the ghost cackled again, delighting in Fuzzy's dilemma. "Reckless you were, and now you will suffer. Ha-ha-ha-ha!"

Fuzzy's heart thumped so hard against his rib cage, he thought it might pound its way out and go bouncing around the jar. His body was stiffer than a stale biscuit, and his tongue felt frozen to the roof of his mouth.

Around his prison the spirit circled, tapping and tapping, while keeping up that bloodcurdling chuckle. His back to the glass, Fuzzy swiveled, watching it. The bitter tang of eucalyptus and fear filled his nostrils.

"Can a rodent diiiie of friiiight?" the ghost crooned. Without waiting for an answer, it boomed, "Let's find out!"

Quick as a lightning strike, it whooshed backward and then rushed the jar, screaming, "Eeeee-*yow*!"

Wheek wheek! Fuzzy sprang straight up in terror. Every hair on his body stood at attention (except the ones smeared with honey). His eyes felt like they were bugging out of his head.

Reduced to a nervous blob, Fuzzy collapsed on the bottom of the jar. "P-p-please," he begged.

"Fuzzarino?" came a voice from above. It sounded like . . .

"Luther!" cried Fuzzy, half rising. "Help! The ghost is after me!"

The spirit noticed the boa peering into the room. In a whirl of white, the phantom spun, gave a little hop, and began to float away.

But then, the oddest thing happened. The ghost's

insubstantial form seemed almost to catch on the edge of the bookshelf. For a moment, it hung there, stuck like a kite in a tree.

It twitched violently—once, twice—and with a sound like a jet ripping past, it zoomed away.

Fuzzy gaped. *What the what?*

"You all right, Fuzzmeister?" Luther's head poked through the mouth of the jar. "Say, you don't look like a spirit to me."

"No, I'm . . ." Fuzzy was still distracted by the ghost's actions. "Did you see that?"

"The gho*ssst*? Weird City, baby. Looked like it caught its booty on the bookshelf."

"Help me out of here," said Fuzzy. He clung to the boa's muscular neck, and with a bit of old-fashioned heave-ho, Luther pulled him from the jar.

Together, they checked out the edge of the bookcase. And there, caught on a hook that held a paper *calavera* cutout, was a scrap of white fabric. Fuzzy retrieved the fragment, and Luther and he gave it a thorough sniffing.

"Whew, eucalyptus!" said Fuzzy. His nose crinkled. "That's strong."

"There's another scent underneath it." As Luther inhaled more deeply, a curious expression crossed his face. "I know that smell."

"What is it?" asked Fuzzy.

A slow smile bloomed on the boa's features. "We've been going at this all wrong."

"We have?" said Fuzzy. "How do you mean?"

"We don't have a ghost problem," said the snake.

"But—"

Luther shook his head. "No way, baby. We got ourselves a *rat* problem."

CHAPTER 11

A Rat in Spook's Clothing

Once a thought lodged itself in Mistletoe's mind, it was like a tick on a warthog's heinie—stubborn as heck and hard to remove. Back at the clubhouse, Fuzzy and Luther spent a good five minutes convincing the mouse that Fuzzy wasn't a ghost pretending to be a guinea pig.

"Posi-tutely?" she asked, hiding under the ramp.

"Absolutely," they said.

At long last, Mistletoe crept out of the shadows. Slowly, carefully, she extended a finger until it poked Fuzzy's belly.

"*Augh*, that tickles!" He twisted away from her touch.

A broad smile wreathed the mouse's face. "That settles it," she said. "Spirits aren't ticklish. Welcome back, Fuzzy."

"Thanks," he said, "I think."

But if they found Mistletoe to be a tough sell, it took even longer to persuade the other pets that 4-B's phantom was actually a flesh-and-blood rat. Igor in particular didn't want to believe that he'd fainted over a simple rodent.

"No way," said the iguana.

"Way," said Fuzzy.

"And you're sure it's not a ghost rat?" asked Marta.

"Positively positive," said Luther. "The nose knows. Mr. Rat doused himself in eucalyptus oil so we wouldn't *sss*mell him. Must have gotten it from Room 4-A, where they're doing an Australia unit."

"Huh. I wondered why 4-B stank like a koala bear's breakfast," mused Sassafras.

"What we've got ourselves," said Luther, "is a rat in spook's clothing."

Cinnabun wrinkled her nose skeptically. "But how do we know for certain?"

"See this?" Fuzzy held up the scrap of sheet. "Spirits

don't have real bodies. But here's a piece of one that caught on a hook."

"A ghost hook?" asked Igor.

"A normal hook," said Fuzzy. "And this 'piece of ghost' smells of eucalyptus and rat."

Cinnabun took a whiff, twitching her nose. "And laundry detergent. Okay, you've convinced me."

Igor came over and sniffed long and deep, muttering to himself.

"That rat had us all bamboozled," said Luther. "*Sss*neaky rodent." He glanced at Fuzzy, Mistletoe, and Cinnabun. "No offense."

"None taken," they said.

"And technically, I'm not a rodent," Cinnabun added.

Shaking his head admiringly, the boa said, "That rat. Pretending to be a phantom, just to scare us off. Now, that's tricky."

"Didn't fool me for a minute." Igor crossed his arms.

Sassafras smirked. "Riiight," she drawled. "Not for a minute—just those thousands of seconds where you fainted from fear."

"Blood sugar imbalance," said the iguana. But he wouldn't meet her eyes.

Mistletoe scratched her head. "But if it's not a ghost, how did it fly?"

Fuzzy and Luther traded a glance, and the snake shrugged. "Probably found some way to hook onto those fake cobwebs," said Luther.

Sassafras's face lit up. "Like zip-lining."

"Excuse me?" said Marta.

"I saw it on TV," said the parakeet. "Humans zip through the trees on a rope line."

"Sounds scary," said the tortoise.

"Nah, they do it all the time in the jungles where I come from."

Igor snorted. "You come from a pet shop on Seventh Avenue."

"I was talking about my *family*," said Sassafras. "Duh."

Mistletoe bit a knuckle. "But what about those glowing footprints? That's gotta be a ghost, right? They looked like humans' shoes."

"*Ssso?*" said Luther. "A rat can't dip its teeny-weeny shoes into glow-in-the-dark paint?"

"And the blue lights?" asked the mouse.

"Just lights," said Fuzzy.

Mistletoe looked like she'd been told an uncomfortable truth about Santa Claus and didn't know how to handle it. "Really, truly?"

"Believe it, baby," said Luther.

With a mighty hop, Cinnabun launched herself up onto the presidential podium. "Brothers and sisters, attention, please. This information casts a whole new light on things."

"You can say that again," mumbled Igor. If a green iguana could have blushed, he'd be red as a cherry tomato kissing a strawberry.

"Now that we know what's really going on," said Cinnabun, "our club has a serious question to consider."

Fuzzy rolled his eyes; her "serious questions" were anything but. "What costume the rat will wear in our parade?" he muttered.

The bunny spun, one paw to her chest. "Why, no, Brother Fuzzy. Before we pick out a costume, I think we should decide what to *do* about the rat. Should it stay or go?"

Everyone spoke at once, voices overlapping.

"Boot it out!"

"Give the rat a chance."

"They're dirty creatures!"

"No dirtier than you."

Bam-bam-bam! Cinnabun whacked the presidential gavel on the podium. "Order! Order!" When the other pets had quieted down, she smoothed the fur on her floppy ears. "My stars, it seems everyone's got an opinion. Let's hear what y'all think before we take a vote. Brother Igor?"

"Wild critters belong in the wild," said the iguana. "They carry diseases and stuff. I say get rid of it."

Marta spoke up. "It's a living creature, just like us. The poor thing probably needs a home. Let it stay."

"Poor thing?" said Igor. "You'll sing a different tune when it gives you rabies, and cooties, and bubonic plague."

"Pretty sure rats don't have cooties," said Cinnabun.

Fuzzy stood. "What about Mr. Darius?"

"I don't think he has cooties either," said Sassafras.

"No, I mean, the rat keeps making a mess in the fourth-grade classrooms, and Mr. Darius has to clean it up," said Fuzzy. "I think we should support our friend and evict the rat."

"Amen, baby," said Luther.

Cinnabun rapped her gavel again. "All right, we've heard some different opinions. Now let's vote. All in favor of letting the rat stay?"

Only Marta raised her front foot.

"And who wants it to leave?"

All the other pets except Mistletoe lifted a paw or tail.

"How about you, Little Bit?" asked Luther.

The mouse shrugged, clearly uncomfortable. "A rat is . . . kind of like a cousin. I really shouldn't vote."

"No problem," said Igor. "Majority rules. The dirty rotten rat must go!"

A few minutes later, all the pets except Marta waited in the crawl space just above Room 4-B. Cinnabun surveyed the group. "Let me do the talking," she said.

Igor bristled. "You don't think I can handle it?"

"I'm sure you could, Brother Igor," said the bunny. "But this might require a more delicate approach."

The iguana puffed out his cheeks. "You saying I'm rude?"

"No, not at—" Cinnabun began.

"Rude, crude, and totally tactless," said Sassafras.

Igor proved the bird's point by sticking out his tongue at her and blowing a raspberry.

Cinnabun cleared her throat. "If we're quite ready . . . ?"

She and Fuzzy lifted the ceiling tile, exposing the darkened classroom below.

Mistletoe gulped. "And we're *sure* it's not a ghost rat?"

Fuzzy patted her on the back reassuringly and dropped down onto the bookcase. One by one, the other pets joined him, making their way to the floor.

"Hello?" called Fuzzy. "Mr. Rat?"

"Or Ms. Rat?" said Cinnabun.

They scanned the deserted room, which smelled of Elmer's glue, eucalyptus, and peanut butter. Nothing moved but the wall clock's second hand.

"My dear rat," said Cinnabun, "we're the classroom pets, come to visit. Might we have a word?"

For a few heartbeats, the room was silent, except for a faint ticking.

"Hey, fat rat!" yelled Igor. Mistletoe and Cinnabun immediately shushed him.

Something rustled on the teacher's desktop. "So," said a raspy voice, "ya finally figured it out? Took ya long enough."

When Fuzzy turned to look, he saw a dark gray rat peeking over the edge of the desk. As he watched, the creature rose onto its hind legs and leaned casually against a cupful of pens and pencils.

"Uh, yes, we saw through your little charade," said Cinnabun, hopping forward. "Allow me to introduce myself. I am—"

"Cinnabun, yeah," said the rat. "I picked that up. Whaddaya want?"

The bunny smoothed her chest fur. "We have come to make a request."

"Well, la-di-dah," said the rat.

"Your being here has caused turmoil in our school," said Cinnabun.

Clapping a paw to his chest, the rat gasped, "Turmoil? Say it ain't so. Yer breaking my heart."

Cinnabun brightened. "Oh, then you won't mind."

The intruder arched an eyebrow. "Mind what?"

"Leaving," said Fuzzy.

Cinnabun rested a paw on his arm. "On behalf of the school," she said, adopting her most adorable expression, "we have come to ask that you kindly move out of Room 4-B and leave Leo Gumpus Elementary."

The rat smiled a wide, friendly smile. "Well, since ya ask so nicely . . ."

"Yes?" The bunny returned his grin.

"No way, Carrot Breath."

The pets gasped.

"Watch it, buster!" Fuzzy bristled. He might tease Cinnabun from time to time, but that didn't mean this stranger could call her names.

The rat jabbed a thumb at himself. "I got dibs on this room, and frankly, it's none of yer beeswax where I live. So kindly butt out."

Cinnabun clapped a paw to her cheek. "Well, I never!"

"I'm sure ya didn't, cupcake," said the rat. "Now, beat it. I got things to do."

Stabbing one of his long fingers at the intruder, Igor said, "Oh, yeah? We can do this the easy way or the hard way, Plague Breath."

"Great, I like the hard way." And with that, the rat knocked over the cup, raining writing utensils down onto the pets.

By the time they'd recovered, he was nowhere to be seen. Luther and Igor searched halfheartedly for the intruder, but quickly gave up. The request had been made; the rat had rejected it. Time to retreat and plan their next move. One by one, the pets began clambering back up the bookcase and into the crawl space.

"This isn't over, Ratface!" called Igor from the top of the bookshelf.

Obnoxious though the iguana might be, Fuzzy knew he was right. Their challenge hadn't ended when they figured out what was haunting Room 4-B.

As a matter of fact, it had only just begun.

CHAPTER 12

A Hint of Mint

Like a snow cone gulped too quickly, the rat was giving the Class Pets Club a colossal collective headache. Maybe they'd gotten too used to having the run of the school, to having things their way. Maybe they were just suspicious of newcomers. Whatever the reason, the pets couldn't ignore him.

They didn't want to think about the rat, and yet he was all they could think about. So after school the next day, the pets gathered in the clubhouse to decide what to do about their uninvited visitor.

Based on their earlier encounters, they knew the rat was clever and not easily intimidated. Driving him out would take some serious brainpower. Fuzzy and his friends hunched on their pillows, frowning, chewing over ideas, and nibbling Power Bars for strength.

"Um, we could . . . smoke him out," said Sassafras.

Igor smirked. "Yeah, 'cause it worked out so well the last time we used fire."

"So what's your bright idea?" The parakeet bristled. "Wearing cat masks and going *meow*?"

Mistletoe shuddered. "Ugh, I hate that sound," she muttered. Then she sat up straighter. "Hey, can I ask a question?"

"That's a question right there," Fuzzy teased.

"Yes, Sister Mistletoe?" said Cinnabun.

The mouse looked around at the other pets. "What've you got against rats, anyway? Geronimo was a rat, and nobody minded him."

Sassafras ruffled her feathers. "Well, there's rats, and then there's *rats*."

"Yeah," said Igor. "I knew Geronimo. I liked Geronimo. And this sneaky little stinker is no Geronimo. He's got to go."

Lazily, Luther uncoiled and stretched. "You know, we're overlooking the easiest solution."

"What's that?" asked Fuzzy.

"I could just eat him. *Gulp, slurp,* problem *sss*olved."

The other pets exchanged uneasy glances. Fuzzy toyed with a whisker.

"What?" asked Luther.

Cinnabun smiled her gentlest smile. "Brother Luther, let's see if we can avoid violence as a solution. It's just so . . . violent."

"Plus, eating someone sets a bad precedent," added Marta.

Luther shrugged, rippling his muscular coils. "Just trying to be helpful."

Eager to change the subject, Fuzzy said, "So help us out, Mistletoe. What do rats absolutely hate?"

"Um, cats and dogs?" said the mouse.

Cinnabun shook her head. "More violence. We can't just turn a cat loose at Leo Gumpus. No telling what it would do."

"Agreed," said Fuzzy, thinking of Miss Tiddy-Bum-Bums.

"We need a plan that doesn't involve someone being eaten," said the bunny.

"Oh." Sassafras straightened. "I'm such a ditz."

"No argument here," said Igor, gnawing on a fruit stick.

Cinnabun shushed him. "What is it, sister?"

Slapping a wing against her forehead, the parakeet said, "I just now remembered something."

"That iguanas are superior in every way to birds?" said Igor.

"In your dreams," said the parakeet. "No, a kid in my class did a report on household pests. Although she didn't mention iguanas"—Sassafras shot a pointed look at Igor—"she did talk about rats."

"And?" said Fuzzy, sitting up.

Sassafras tilted her head back, remembering. "I think she said that they hate the smell of those cakes in the little boys' room."

"They've got cake in the bathroom?" Mistletoe frowned. "How did I miss that?"

"Not birthday cake," said the parakeet. "De-stinkifying cake. They put it in the . . . you know."

"Eeeww." Cinnabun grimaced. "I'm not touching one of those things for love or clover."

"Me neither," said Fuzzy. The other pets registered their disgust.

"Did that girl's report say anything els*sss*e?" asked Luther.

Sassafras nodded. "She also said rats hate the smell of mint."

"Mint?" said Marta. "You can't be serious."

"It's true," said Mistletoe. "We mice don't like it either."

Getting to his feet, Fuzzy said, "Okay, mint we can do. Miss Wills keeps a couple boxes of those mint cookies in her desk to reward good students."

"I'll help," said Igor quickly. "I *love* mint."

Fuzzy hesitated. The iguana had a tendency to munch anything that came within arm's reach, and Fuzzy had to wonder whether the cookies would survive the trip. He raised his eyebrows at Luther, who caught his meaning.

"No need, Iggy-baby," said the snake. "Me and the Fuzzmeister have got this covered."

"That's right," said Fuzzy.

Igor's expression of disappointment was almost comical. "Well . . . if you're sure . . ."

"Sure we're sure." Fuzzy clapped his paws together. "No time like the present, eh, Luther?"

"Lead on, Fuzzarino," said the snake.

* * *

Without someone trying to eat their cargo, it was a breeze for the two pets to carry a half-cylinder of mint cookies to Room 4-B. Luther and Fuzzy left the treats where they thought the rat would be most likely to smell them. Checking around, they found no sign of the intruder. *Off somewhere causing mischief, no doubt,* thought Fuzzy.

He gnawed his lip. Taking Miss Wills's cookies was wrong, Fuzzy knew, and he also knew she'd probably blame her students. That wasn't good. But on the plus side, the teacher never held a grudge for long. And besides, Fuzzy told himself that the benefits for 4-B's students far outweighed the inconvenience for his own kids.

Still, his conscience throbbed like an infected molar.

On their way out, Fuzzy and Luther paused atop the bookcase for a while, watching for any signs of the rat.

"Why mint?" said Luther at last.

"How's that?" asked Fuzzy.

"Why is it *mint* that rats hate? Why not coffee, or cupcake*sss*, or broccoli?"

Fuzzy lifted a shoulder. "One of nature's little mysteries, I guess."

As he threaded through the crawl space back to his own classroom, Fuzzy was surprised to feel a flash of sympathy for the unwanted visitor. Maybe Marta was right. Maybe the rat, obnoxious though he was, just needed a home.

Catching himself, Fuzzy tightened his jaw. The students' needs had to come first, now and always. That rat wasn't good for the kids or the school, so he had to go. After all, he could easily find a home somewhere else.

Right?

Settling down in his igloo to sleep, Fuzzy knew they were making the correct move, forcing the rat to leave. But one thing nagged at him:

If it was so right, why did it feel so wrong?

CHAPTER 13

Pig in a Tutu?

Only three school days remained before the costume parade. In Fuzzy's class, Halloween spirit was running higher than a squirrel up a redwood tree. Nearly everyone had chosen his or her costume, except for Ryan-with-the-glasses, who could never make up his mind. Fuzzy fully expected that Ryan's would be the first zombie-pirate-wolfman-Spider-Man outfit the school had ever seen.

Still feeling conflicted about driving out the rat, Fuzzy seesawed between sureness and guilt. Luckily, the festive atmosphere made for a handy distraction.

Students laughed and joked as they made papier-mâché skulls and left them to dry. Now that he knew the school wasn't haunted, Fuzzy could relax and enjoy how creepy and Halloweeny Room 5-B had become. With *calaveras*, ghosts, and goblins galore, the place looked spookier than a wagonload of witches at midnight.

But it wasn't quite complete.

"Hey, Miss Wills," said Zoey-with-the-braces. "We forgot something."

"What's that?" asked the teacher, directing the papier-mâché cleanup.

"It's Fuzzy," said Zoey. "He doesn't have a costume yet."

Fuzzy stiffened. This wasn't strictly true. He'd borrowed a Batman cape and mask from some fourth grader's diorama and hidden it away, planning to attend the pets' costume contest as the Caped Crusader.

"Fuz-zy, Fuz-zy!" chanted Loud Brandon.

"Let's dress him up as a skunk," said Heavy-Handed Jake.

A skunk? Fuzzy grimaced. Couldn't his students come up with something cooler, more adventurous? Surely one of the girls . . . ?

"No, he should be a cutesy-wutesy ladybug," said Abby.

A grinning Sofia said, "No, a ballerina. I've even got the tutu."

Fuzzy gave a soft *wheek*. So much for the girls' ideas. Bad enough that Miss Wills's class from two years back had named him Fuzzy instead of Rex, Killer, or something more macho.

But to be stuck wearing a tutu? That was more than a boar guinea pig could bear.

He reared up onto his hind legs and placed his paws on his hips, trying to look like a superhero. Maybe that would help the kids get the right idea.

Amir spotted him. "Hey, Fuzzy's looking nice and plump. Maybe he should be a hot dog."

The class burst out laughing. Fuzzy deflated. These poor kids couldn't even recognize a superhero when one was staring them in the face.

"He's your pet," Maya told Miss Wills. "What costume do *you* want him to wear?"

"Well, I always think of Fuzzy as *our* pet. But . . ." The teacher crossed to the cage and cocked her head, considering. "I believe our friend would be happiest without too much stuff on him. He needs a simple costume."

No fooling, thought Fuzzy, who'd been picturing himself all wrapped up in a hot dog bun and covered with relish. He gazed at Miss Wills, hoping she could read his mind.

"Maybe we should make Fuzzy a . . . shark," said the teacher. "That way, all he has to wear is a fin."

The kids cheered. Fuzzy blinked. Oh well. At least a shark was scary.

When lunchtime rolled around, Fuzzy was tempted to sneak over to Room 4-B and see whether their minty assault had scared off the intruder yet. But since the rat would probably lay low during school hours, he decided to do the same. After school would have to be soon enough.

A few hours later, Miss Wills ended the day by turning on some funny music and teaching the students how to dance the Monster Mash. Fuzzy kept looking around for mushed-up creatures, but the dance turned out to involve lots of twisting and making scary faces. Finally, the bell rang, and the kids headed home. After dropping a few pumpkin seeds into Fuzzy's food dish, Miss Wills followed them.

But just as she reached the door, it opened. In

stepped Mr. Darius with a scowling Mrs. Drone right on his heels.

"I'm glad I caught you," said the janitor. "We have a problem in a couple of the fourth-grade classrooms, and I was wondering if you had it too."

"Had what?" asked Miss Wills, brushing her brown bangs off her forehead.

"Rats," growled Mrs. Drone. "We've got filthy, rotten *rats!*"

The teacher put a hand to her chest. "Here at school?"

"Over in 4-B and 4-A, we found some shredded papers, gnawed wires—" Mr. Darius began.

"And scat!" added Mrs. Drone.

"What scat?" said Miss Wills.

"Rat scat."

"Fancy that."

Mr. Darius nodded. "Plus, we found cookie crumbs all over the classroom."

Fuzzy frowned. It sounded like this rat wasn't bothered by mint at all.

There goes another good idea . . . he thought.

"Cookie crumbs?" said the teacher. "You know, now that you mention it, some of the cookies in my desk went missing." Fuzzy felt his ears grow warm. *Oops.*

"Have you seen any other signs of rat activity?" Mr. Darius asked.

"Anything at all?" his assistant chimed in eagerly.

Miss Wills shook her head. "Everything else is the same as normal."

Fuzzy noticed that Mrs. Drone seemed almost disappointed. Strange. But then, there was no accounting for humans.

Running a hand over his buzzed-short hair, Mr. Darius said, "Maybe kids took your cookies—"

"Maybe not," said Mrs. Drone.

"But let me know if anything changes. Or if you see any other rat signs."

The assistant janitor's face clenched like an angry fist. "We should nuke the whole place, just to be sure."

Miss Wills gasped.

"Rhonda, you know we can't set out poison at school." Mr. Darius narrowed his eyes. "It's not safe."

"Oh, and rats *are*? Their diseases can kill people, you know. Important people," Mrs. Drone added, almost to herself.

The janitor turned to Miss Wills. "Not to worry. We've laid some traps to see if we can't nip this rat invasion in the bud."

Traps? Fuzzy couldn't suppress a shocked chirp.

"Gosh, do you have to?" The teacher's forehead crinkled. "Those poor creatures are only trying to survive. They don't deserve to be killed."

Fuzzy had to agree. He felt a queasy twinge in his belly at the thought that those mint cookies might indirectly lead to the rat's death. The pets had only wanted to drive the intruder away, not bump him off.

Mr. Darius smiled. "Relax. I'm using humane traps."

Mrs. Drone glowered. "Over my strenuous objections."

The look Mr. Darius sent her was chillier than a penguin's lunchbox. "Let's try to remember who's the assistant here and who's the janitor."

Her arms folded and her lower lip pushed out, but Mrs. Drone made no reply.

"So you see, Miss Wills," the janitor continued, turning his back on his assistant, "the rats won't even get hurt." When the teacher still looked doubtful, he said, "I know it doesn't seem fair, but I have to catch them. It's a safety issue."

"Are you worried about rat bites?" asked Miss Wills. Fuzzy listened closer.

"Worse than that, it's gnawing on wires," said Mr. Darius. "And if it munches the wrong one, and the wire sparks? *Foom!*" His big hands spread wide. "This whole school could go up in flames."

Fuzzy gave a start. Who knew the rat posed that big of a risk? This was a much more serious problem than merely making messes and spreading diseases. Something must be done. Still, Fuzzy wished there was a gentler way to deal with their unwanted visitor.

"Well, I suppose you know what's best," said Miss Wills.

Patting her arm, Mr. Darius said, "Trust me. When it comes to dirt, messes, and pests, I'm the man with the plan."

Miss Wills chuckled a little, wished the custodians good night, and slipped out the door. With a final glare at her supervisor, Mrs. Drone followed her.

The janitor just shook his head.

With wide eyes, Fuzzy watched the man sweep up and empty the wastebaskets. He was glad that the humans were helping to get rid of the rat, but something just didn't feel right about their plan. Fuzzy wondered what would happen to the rat after he was caught. Would he be tossed out on the street or sent to some kind of rat jail?

Even the slice of carrot that Mr. Darius slipped him didn't erase Fuzzy's worry. He retreated to his igloo to chew and ponder.

By the time the janitor left the room, Fuzzy had a plan. He would leave immediately, find the rat, and warn him about the traps. Maybe if the intruder realized how serious the humans were, he would leave on his own before getting caught.

Would his plan work? Fuzzy didn't know.

But it was worth a try.

Bristling with purpose, Fuzzy climbed out of his cage and scaled the bookcase up into the crawl space.

He hoped he wasn't too late. Through the dusty drop ceiling he trotted, dodging around ducts and wiring.

Before long, Fuzzy hung and dropped softly into Room 4-B.

"Mr. Rat?" he called. "You there?" Fuzzy scrambled down the bookshelves. "We need to talk; it's important."

The room was as quiet as an undertaker's whisper. Fuzzy scanned the teacher's desk. No rat. He checked the stack of construction paper. Still no rat. Finally, Fuzzy headed over to the corner, where he noticed the closet door was ajar.

He pushed it open. "Mr. Rat? Hello? You've got to get out of here. They're setting traps for you."

Faint, fading light from the windows barely illuminated the little closet. Fuzzy searched for the rat's nest. He pawed through plastic bins, rolled-up papers, and an old pair of Mrs. Sanchez's boots. And then . . .

Sniff-sniff. The most delightful smell. Sweet and nutty and altogether yummy.

Following his nose over to the right back corner, Fuzzy noticed a silver wire contraption about the size of a breadbox. The good smell was coming from deep inside it.

Cautiously, Fuzzy edged forward. He sniffed the metal and caught a whiff of Mr. Darius's scent. Fuzzy relaxed at the smell of his buddy. He padded into the contraption, which, now that he thought of it, looked kind of like a small cage.

The yummy odor arose from a glob at the far end. The closer he got, the more delicious it smelled. Trotting over to it, Fuzzy began nibbling.

Mmm. So smooth, so creamy . . .

Whang!

Something clanged behind him. Whirling, Fuzzy discovered that a metal plate had blocked off his escape.

Holy haystacks!

He was trapped.

CHAPTER 14

Well and Truly Trapped

Wheek, wheek! Fuzzy tore around inside the trap, panic burning a hole in his gut.

"Hey!" he squealed, gripping the bars. "Let me out!"

Fuzzy rushed over to the metal plate and tried shoving it aside, but the darned thing wouldn't budge.

"Somebody, help!" he cried. "I'm not supposed to be here!"

A sarcastic chuckle drifted down from somewhere above him. Craning his neck, Fuzzy saw a dark-gray figure hop off the lowest shelf and scramble down the plastic bins.

"Sucker," said the rat.

"Can you help me?" asked Fuzzy.

The furry intruder sauntered over to the cage, picked up a stray paper clip, and chewed on it. "Why should I? Whattaya ever done for me?"

"I came here to warn you about the traps," said Fuzzy.

The rat snorted, rapping the metal plate with a knuckle. "Yeah, I knew about them before you did, Chubby Cheeks. Only a total yo-yo gets caught in one of these."

Fuzzy's ears grew warm. "I, uh, never saw a trap before."

"Uh-huh. So ya just waltzed on inside looking for peanut butter."

Fuzzy lifted a shoulder. "Actually, I walked." With a paw, he scooped up some of the goop and stuffed it into his mouth. "So this is—*mmf*—what peanut butter tastes like? De-*mmf*-licious."

"Worth being in the slammer for?" said the rat.

Licking the last of the creamy mess off his fingers, Fuzzy said, "Not really. Look, Mr. Rat—um, I can't keep calling you that. What's your name?"

"Vinnie," said the rat. "And you're Fuzzy, right?"

Fuzzy blinked. "How did you—?"

"Oh, please," said Vinnie. "No secrets in this school. I creep around just as much as you guys do."

"Vinnie, could you please let me out of here?" Fuzzy didn't have Cinnabun's adorability skills, but he tried to look as friendly as he could.

The rat cocked his head. "Could I? Probably. What's in it for me?"

"My undying gratitude and the friendship of the Class Pets Club?"

"Ha!" Vinnie threw up his paws and spun on his heel. "Later, Piggie Pie." He tossed the paper clip and began striding away.

"Wait!" Fuzzy gripped the bars.

The rat stopped. "I'm listening."

"What's wrong with friendship and gratitude?"

Turning, Vinnie swaggered back toward the trap. "Friendship? From a bunch of pampered pets who just want to toss me out into the snow?"

"Snow?" said Fuzzy. "It's only October."

The rat rolled his eyes. "Ya miss my point. You and yer pals ain't exactly rolled out the welcoming mat."

Fuzzy frowned. Vinnie was right, at least partly. "But you haven't been friendly either—pretending to be a ghost, trying to scare us."

"Self-defense!" sputtered the rat, jabbing a finger at

Fuzzy's chest. "From the second I saw that dingbat Mistletoe, I knew you pets would try to run me off. Was I right or was I right?"

Fuzzy opened his mouth and then shut it. Arguing wouldn't help him break out of the trap. And he very much needed to break out. If 4-B's teacher, Mrs. Sanchez, found him here, she'd tell Mr. Darius that Fuzzy was an escape artist.

And that would be that.

No more freedom, no more Class Pets Club meetings.

"So what do you want?" he asked.

"To be left alone to enjoy this sweet crib," said Vinnie.

Fuzzy cocked his head. "But you're a *wild* rat," he said. "I thought you guys just nested in trees and stuff."

"What are ya, the Nature Channel?"

Fuzzy gave a half shrug. He'd actually seen that tidbit about rats on National Geographic.

Vinnie snorted again. "Why do you pets automatically assume I'm wild?"

"You're not?"

"Pass me some peanut butter, and I'll set ya straight," said the rat.

Fuzzy obeyed, settling in to listen.

"I used to be a pampered pet, ya know," Vinnie began, slurping the gooey treat from his fingers. "For a whole freakin' year. Life wasn't so bad with old Mr. Herman. Fed me. Taught me some tricks. But then, things changed."

"What do you mean?" asked Fuzzy.

"Mr. Herman started dressing me up in costumes," said Vinnie.

Fuzzy smiled. "Sounds fun."

"Yeah, once or twice," said Vinnie. "But then the guy got nutso about it. He wouldn't quit. You try being a slice of pizza one day, a bumblebee the next, and a taco the day after that."

"A taco?"

Vinnie shook his head, disgusted. "It was like Halloween every freakin' day. When he dressed me up as Pope Ratty the First, Herman even gave me shoes."

"So *that's* how you made those ghost footprints," said Fuzzy.

Running a paw through his shaggy fur, the rat shuddered. "I tell ya, I was starting to lose my self-respect. So I ran away."

"Aw, you're a pet without a home," said Fuzzy.

"Yeah, yeah, spare me the violins." Vinnie rubbed his cheek and turned away, pretending to study a plastic bin.

Fuzzy's throat tightened. It was one of the saddest things he'd ever heard. He couldn't imagine being separated from Miss Wills and how awful that would feel. Fuzzy wanted to help the rat, but he couldn't see how.

"Don't you miss Mr. Herman?" said Fuzzy.

"That knucklehead?" Vinnie scoffed. "No, but I miss the good life. Comfy place to sleep, plenty of snuggles, all meals provided—ya don't know how easy ya got it here."

Hmm, thought Fuzzy, *he actually likes snuggles*. The beginnings of an idea started forming in Fuzzy's mind, glimmering like faint stars at twilight. "What if . . . what if I could find you a home?"

"Got one right here," said Vinnie. "4-B's been good to me. Snacks in the teacher's desk, water in the sink, plenty of paper for my nest. Plus, no classroom pet to give me grief." He shot a significant glance at Fuzzy. "Until you guys showed up."

Fuzzy rose. "Yeah, but you can't stay."

"Oh, ya gonna kick me out, Parsley Breath?" Vinnie puffed out his chest.

"Not me," said Fuzzy. "Mr. Darius knows about you now, and he won't stop until he catches you."

"Ha!" Vinnie smirked. "I wish him luck. Ain't a trap been made that can hold Vinnie T. Rat."

"But is this how you want to live?"

"Sure, why not?"

"Really?" Fuzzy met the rat's eyes. "Always on the lookout, skulking in the shadows? Always afraid of being seen? Wouldn't you like an easier life, with a human to take care of you?"

A shadow of doubt crossed Vinnie's face. Fuzzy pressed his advantage.

"Get me out of this trap, and I'll help you find a home," said Fuzzy. "Please?"

For a long moment, Vinnie considered the offer. He squinted ferociously, and Fuzzy could practically see him weighing the pros and cons.

"Deal," said the rat at last.

"That's great!" chirped Fuzzy.

"But." Vinnie held up a finger. "I swear, if this is some kind of trick—if ya back out on our deal, you'll be the sorriest piggy that ever drew breath."

"I'm a rodent, actually," said Fuzzy. "Like you."

"So's a porcupine, but ya won't catch me cuddling one." Vinnie scowled. "I'm warning ya, family ties count for zip."

Fuzzy raised a paw. "I swear I'm not trying to trick you. I just want to help."

"*And* get out of the trap," said Vinnie.

"That too."

With a last grumble, the rat bent and gripped a silver loop on the other side of the metal plate. "When I give the signal, push on the bottom of that door with all yer might. Ready?"

Fuzzy braced a shoulder against the metal. "Ready."

"Push!" The rat strained upward and Fuzzy shoved as hard as he could. "Harder!" Vinnie grunted. His teeth were clenched, and the wiry muscles stood out in his arms.

Digging in his paws and straining forward, Fuzzy tried to oblige. "This—*ugh*—is as hard as it—*ugh*—gets."

The door lifted maybe a quarter of an inch, then slammed shut with a *clack*. Fuzzy slumped to the floor. Vinnie cursed, shaking his paws to work the feeling back into them.

"Almost . . . had it," Fuzzy panted. "Let's . . . try again."

Glaring at the contraption, the rat planted his fists on his hips. "No trap gets the best of me. This time, we're doing it smarter."

"How?" asked Fuzzy.

"With leverage," said Vinnie. He eyeballed the stack of plastic bins beside them and glanced at the shelf above. Then, scrambling up, he popped the lid of the topmost bin. After a bit of rummaging, he pulled from it a roll of twine.

As Fuzzy watched, the rat tied one end to the loop on the trap's door, climbed with the ball to a high shelf, and draped the twine over a sturdy hook. Then Vinnie tossed down the ball and peered over the edge. He gave the twine a couple of strong yanks.

"All right," said Vinnie. "When I make like Tarzan, push that door with all yer piggy might. Got it?"

"Got it. But what are you—?"

"Here we go," said the rat. "*Uno* . . . *dos* . . . three!"

As Vinnie swung off the shelf gripping one end of the twine, Fuzzy shoved against the metal plate with a mighty "*Gnnnuff!*"

For a moment, the door seemed stuck. But then, with a squeak, it moved! Between Vinnie's weight lifting the plate and Fuzzy's push-push-pushing, the door lifted just enough for him to squeeze through the gap.

Pwanngg!

The plate slammed shut so close behind him that if guinea pigs had tails, Fuzzy would've lost his. He collapsed to the floor, quivering.

Sliding down the twine, Vinnie landed beside him. "After all that work," said the rat, "my new home better be a regular Taj Mahal."

CHAPTER 15

Big Ugly's Big Idea

Leading the way back to the clubhouse, Fuzzy found his legs were still rubbery. That had been a bit too close of a call, even for the Class Pets director of adventure. Fuzzy vowed to avoid all traps and peanut butter in the future.

Well, maybe not peanut butter.

Vinnie said not a word until they were approaching the ramp that led down into the clubhouse. He caught Fuzzy's arm. "Maybe you should go in first to pave the way."

"What do you mean?" said Fuzzy.

"I ain't exactly their sweet patootie," said the rat.

"Did ya forget? For the past week, you and yer buddies have tried everything possible to get rid of me."

Fuzzy waved a paw. "No worries. That was then, this is now. My fellow pets are peaceful and understanding."

With a shrug, Vinnie fell in behind as Fuzzy proceeded down the ramp.

"Hey, guys!" called Fuzzy. "I finally made it. And look who I—"

"The rat!" Igor sprang to his feet, eyes narrowing. "That lowdown, dirty rat!"

"Let's get him!" squawked Sassafras.

Behind him, Fuzzy heard Vinnie mutter, "Peaceful and understanding?"

"They just need time," said Fuzzy. He held up his paws to stop Igor, who was heading up the ramp. "Guys, wait! I—"

"Watch out!" cried Marta. "He's got diseases!"

"Take that back, ya walking wrinkle factory!" yelled Vinnie.

"How rude!" huffed the tortoise.

Voices rose as all the pets chimed in, shouting over one another.

Fuzzy's chest felt as tight as a prom dress on a warthog. "Please, will you just listen to me?"

"Who needs to lisssten?" said Luther, slithering closer. "Gulp, slurp, bye-bye, Ratty."

"*STOP!*" bellowed Fuzzy.

The advancing pets paused, startled by his shout.

"Nobody's gulping anybody," said Fuzzy. He clenched his fists. "If you want to get at Vinnie, you'll have to go through me first."

"*Vinnie?*" said Cinnabun.

The rat sketched a salute. "At yer service, Carrot Breath."

With a weary headshake, Marta said, "Never name them. It only makes them harder to get rid of."

"Vinnie is a pet, just like us," said Fuzzy. "He's not some random rat." Then, standing on the ramp between his friends and the homeless pet, he proceeded to tell Vinnie's story. He explained why the rat ran away from home and how his cleverness had rescued Fuzzy from Mr. Darius's trap.

"Well, sure," said Sassafras, "but there wouldn't have been a trap in the first place if he hadn't moved in."

"Totally uninvited." Igor sneered.

"Oh, yeah?" Vinnie matched his sneer. "I cordially invite *you* to meet my *fist*."

"I ought to turn you inside out and wear you for a hat," growled the iguana.

Vinnie snorted. "Ah, yer just sore because I made ya faint with a piece of sheet, a zip line, and some eucalyptus oil." His grin turned mocking. "Dearie me, a ghost!"

"Why, you—"

"Gentlemen, please." Cinnabun raised her paws in a calming gesture. "Can't we discuss this like civilized animals, without all the threats?"

The iguana gave a grudging nod. Vinnie muttered, "He started it." But at Cinnabun's reproachful look, they both settled down.

"I told Vinnie I'd help find him a new home," said Fuzzy, "since he can't go back to his old one."

"Well, he can't stay here," said Sassafras.

"Why not?"

The bird ticked off reasons on her feathers. "(A) He makes a mess; (B) he's got diseases—"

"Hey, I'm sitting right here," said Vinnie. "I can hear ya."

"And (C) he's gonna chew through wires and burn the whole school down."

Fuzzy drew himself up, counting right back at her. "(A) He won't make a mess if we find him a proper home; (B) he's a normal pet, so he doesn't have diseases." He turned to the rat. "You don't, do you?"

"Clean as a whistle," said Vinnie.

"And (C) . . ." Fuzzy paused. This would be trickier. "Vinnie, if you're going to live here, you can't chew on wires anymore."

"But they give me a real kick," said the rat.

"Kick or not, if you're going to be a class pet, you have to swear to protect all students," said Fuzzy. "I think not burning down their school falls under that category."

"Hold the phone." Vinnie leaned back, squinting suspiciously. "Whattaya mean *be a class pet*?"

"That's how we can find you a home," said Fuzzy.

"I never agreed to that," said the rat.

Sassafras snapped, "You want to make him one of *us*? We don't know anything about this . . . this *rodent*."

"Hey," said Fuzzy, Mistletoe, and Cinnabun together, "what's wrong with rodents?"

"Nothing," said Sassafras, backing down.

"Darn tootin'," said Mistletoe.

Igor crossed his arms. "I don't know about this."

"What's the problem?" asked Fuzzy.

The iguana jerked his chin at Vinnie. "For two days, we do our best to get rid of this chump, and now we're supposed to welcome him with hugs and kisses?"

"Who you calling chump, Turkey Neck?" said Vinnie.

"You're rude," said Igor. "I like that. But Sassafras is right; we have to protect the kids."

Fuzzy tried another tack. "Look, what if we took some time and got to know him?"

Putting up his paws, Vinnie said, "Whoa, ya mean holding hands and long walks in the park? Ya got the wrong rat."

"What did you have in mind?" Cinnabun asked Fuzzy.

He descended the ramp and began to pace. Vinnie followed, stopping at the plank's edge to eye the other pets warily. Spotting a pencil stub lying on the floor, the rat picked it up and gnawed on it.

"I was thinking," said Fuzzy, "what if he stays in here for a couple of days while we all get to know one another?"

"In our clubhouse?" said Luther. "I don't know, Fuzzmeister. I'm as cool as the next reptile, but rats tend to poop all over the joint."

"Hey!" Vinnie frowned. "Rats are very clean animals."

"Except when they poop," said the boa.

The rat shrugged. "Everybody poops." He went back to chewing.

"Even Geronimo," said Mistletoe. "And everyone was just fine with him."

Igor avoided her gaze.

Turning to Vinnie, Fuzzy said, "If we let you stay in here, would you agree to do your business outside, in the crawl space?"

"I could do that," said Vinnie. "*If* I stay here."

Sassafras edged closer. "But what about the gnawing?"

Lowering his pencil, the rat said, "What, ya mean my hobby?"

"You can't be chewing on wires or wrecking our clubhouse," said the parakeet.

Vinnie brandished the pencil. "I'll have you know, birdie, I got a condition."

"You're terminally annoying?" said Igor, smirking.

The rat glared. "My teeth don't stop growing, Dragon Face. If I didn't chew on something regularly, they'd grow right through my brain."

"Such a shame." Igor gave the words a sarcastic twist.

Tossing aside the pencil, Vinnie squared his shoulders. "You wanna piece of me, Big Ugly?"

"Oh yeah." Igor rose to his full height, towering above the rat.

Cinnabun pushed between them. "Now, now, gentlemen. We're just having a discussion. No need to get physical."

Igor smiled. "Actually, I just thought of a way to settle this fair and square by *getting* physical."

"What's that?" asked Fuzzy. He didn't like the look in the iguana's eye.

"If Rat Boy here can beat me at arm wrestling, I'm willing to let him stay. If he loses, he leaves."

The rat chuckled. "I won't."

Ignoring him, Igor asked, "Sassafras, is that cool with you?"

The bird nodded. "Hunky-dory. Especially since he won't beat you in a million years."

Cinnabun cocked her head, considering. "And how about the rest of y'all?" she asked. "If Brother Vinnie beats Brother Igor, will you let him stay in the clubhouse while we figure out a better solution?"

One by one, the other pets agreed. At first, Fuzzy resisted. Given the iguana's height and weight advantage, it didn't seem like a fair contest. But he finally said, "If it's okay with Vinnie, it's okay by me."

"What do you say, Brother Vinnie?" asked Cinnabun.

The rat took his time. He scanned the room, noting the pillows, the snacks, the cozy decor. Then he gave the same careful scrutiny to the iguana. "Deal," he said at last. "Ya got a sweet crib here. I could fit right in."

Igor snorted. "Sure. *If* you get through me first, and that's a mighty big *if*."

A small smile played over Vinnie's lips. "Let's find out, Turkey Neck."

CHAPTER 16

In Arms' Way

The pets cleared back as Sassafras stepped out and claimed the center of the space. "Gather 'round, ladies and germs," she squawked. "And place your bets for the fight of the century!"

Fuzzy arched an eyebrow. "Really? Nobody here has lived for a century."

"Yeah, but 'fight of the week' doesn't have the same ring."

Cinnabun and Fuzzy carted over a small wooden box that the pets had been using for a table. They set it up in the middle, and Vinnie and Igor knelt on either side. Luther slithered up next to them.

"Get ready," said the snake.

The iguana and rat planted their elbows on the box and gripped each other's hands. Noticing how much longer and thicker Igor's forearm was, Fuzzy bit his lip. The rat would lose badly, and nothing Fuzzy could do would help. Soon, the poor guy would be back out on the streets, scrabbling for a meal.

"No biting, no scratching, and you start when you hear me say *go*," said Luther. "Both you dudes cool with the rules?"

"Cool as a Popsicle," said Vinnie, looking remarkably calm.

Igor smirked. "This is gonna be so easy." The other pets closed around them in a circle, watching avidly.

"All righty then," said the snake. "Ready . . . set . . ."

By the time the words "Go, baby!" had left his lips, Vinnie had whipped Igor's arm down, nearly to the tabletop. The iguana's eyes popped in alarm. Gritting his teeth, he strained with all his might and just managed to stop the rat from defeating him in two seconds flat.

"Get him, Igor!" cried Sassafras.

"Go, Vinnie!" yelled Fuzzy. The other pets shouted encouragement, shoving forward for a better view.

Veins bulged in Igor's forehead as he tried to work his arm back toward vertical. He won an inch, then another.

Vinnie's jaw clenched, and the rat redoubled his efforts.

For a few moments, the linked fists wavered back and forth. Then Fuzzy noticed a crafty look cross the rat's face. Vinnie's paw slipped further down Igor's palm, until he was mostly grabbing the iguana's fingers. When he squeezed, Igor's mouth dropped open in an O of surprise.

Then the rat curled his wrist, forcing Igor's arm into a weaker angle. He gave a loud grunt.

Thwack! The back of Igor's paw hit the table.

Half of the pets cheered; the other half went, "awww." Fuzzy noted that Vinnie's approval rating was improving.

"And the winner is . . . Vinnie T. Rat!" Luther announced.

Grumbling, the iguana allowed Sassafras to lead him away from the table. Vinnie stood, massaging his biceps and grinning like a jack-o'-lantern.

Rushing up to the rat, Mistletoe gushed, "That was splen-diddley! He's so big, and you're so much smaller. How did you beat him?"

"Simple, Short Stuff," said Vinnie, with a wink at Fuzzy. "Leverage."

Fuzzy shook his head wonderingly. This rat was full of surprises. He didn't know how much longer Vinnie would stay at Leo Gumpus Elementary, but he did know one thing:

Life would never be dull as long as the rat was around.

Fuzzy would have reached Monday's club meeting sooner if he hadn't been sidetracked by some bad news. Just as he had decided that Mr. Darius wasn't coming to clean up and had begun arranging his blocks and ball to escape, loud voices barked right outside the door.

Shoving his ball away, Fuzzy assumed an innocent expression.

Whump!

The door swung open so hard it thunked into the wall and bounced back. In stomped Mr. Darius and Mrs. Drone. To say that neither one looked happy would be like calling World War II a little game of patty-cake.

"—can't believe you went around me like that," the janitor fumed as he entered.

"Well, *you* weren't getting the job done," snapped his assistant. "Somebody had to."

Mr. Darius began sweeping hard enough to peel the tile up off the floor. "But telling Principal Flake about it was *way* out of line. You're on thin ice."

Snatching up a wastebasket like it had slapped her baby, Mrs. Drone *whapped* its contents into the larger bin. "She's my neighbor," snarled the woman. "She asked, and I told her. And now, at least, I've gotten the go-ahead to get rid of those slimy rats for good—*my* way."

Wiggling whiskers!

Fuzzy pushed forward against the cage bars to listen. What had she done?

"I can't believe Mrs. Flake approved this," Mr. Darius growled.

"Believe it," his assistant shot back. "She said to do whatever it takes to resolve the problem."

"But she didn't mean we should go that far." The janitor shoved the dirt onto his dustpan and banged it into the bin. "Using poison and kill traps is *not* how we do things at Leo Gumpus."

"That's right," squeaked Fuzzy.

"It is now," said Mrs. Drone, dumping the second trash can. "And you can bet I'll be on the hunt all day, all night, until the vermin are dead and gone." Her face creased in a mean grin. "Heck, Principal Flake will be so grateful, maybe she'll make *me* head custodian."

And with that, she pushed her way out the door with her wheeled trash bin.

"I'm not done with you!" the janitor snouted.

Muttering to himself, Mr. Darius snatched up his broom and dustpan and stomped out after his assistant. He was so upset, he didn't even stop to give Fuzzy his usual treat.

Uh-oh. That meant, as Fuzzy knew, that things were serious.

Escaping the cage in his usual way, Fuzzy hustled over to the pets' temporary meeting place in a kindergarten classroom.

"You won't believe what I just heard," he blurted. Hopping down onto the elevated play area that the pets had commandeered, he joined the others.

"They're making a movie of my life, and they want Brad Pitt to *ss*star?" Luther's grin was teasing.

"This is serious, Luther," said Fuzzy. "That new assistant janitor has set out deadly traps and poison. She means to kill Vinnie!"

"So?" said Igor.

"*So?!*" Fuzzy bristled. "He's a fellow pet."

"He's sneaky, he's sly, and I don't like him!"

"Oh, I see." Fuzzy lifted his eyebrows. "Is somebody a sore loser?"

The iguana stuck out his tongue in answer.

With Vinnie now living large in their clubhouse, the Class Pets had been forced to meet elsewhere. This kindergarten classroom was the popular choice. Its napping mats were made for comfy seating, and its students could always be relied on to leave plenty of snack crumbs in random places.

Under Cinnabun's guidance, the pets discussed the latest development.

Despite the serious threat of poison, Sassafras and Igor were all for booting out Vinnie as soon as possible. Luther was on the fence. The rest of the pets wanted to find a place for the rat at school or in a loving home.

"Hey, I posted a note in the teachers' lounge on Friday," said Igor. *"Free pet rat, take him away now!"*

"And?" said Sassafras.

"No response yet."

"Aw, rats aren't so bad," said Marta, nibbling on a wilted bit of lettuce she'd found in a toy box. "Geronimo was a rat, and he was our president."

"Completely different situation," said Igor. "He wasn't obnoxious."

"Or an arm-wrestling champ," Mistletoe teased.

The iguana glowered.

Grooming her shoulder fur, Cinnabun said, "Can you picture being homeless? Bless his heart, I can't imagine what poor Brother Vinnie must be feeling right now. No wonder he's acting out."

"That dude would be rude even if he lived in a mansion," said Luther. "A tiger doesn't change his stripes."

Mistletoe frowned. "But Vinnie doesn't *have* stripes."

The snake rolled his eyes. "Figure of speech."

"I just wish we could find a family to adopt him," said the bunny. "But with Vinnie running around loose, he seems less like a pet and more like a pest."

"Got that right," said Sassafras.

Marta tilted her head. "If only we could change his image."

Change his image? Fuzzy sat up straight. "Wait a minute, I just had an idea."

"There's a first time for everything," said Igor.

Ignoring him, Fuzzy said, "The big Halloween costume parade is tomorrow, right?"

"Right," said Mistletoe.

"What if we put a costume on Vinnie?" said Fuzzy. "If the kids and teachers saw him in something cute, he'd seem more like a pet."

Cinnabun nodded slowly, considering. "And then, someone would want to adopt him. Brother Fuzzy, that's brilliant!"

"Oh, I don't know . . ." said Sassafras.

The bunny batted her eyes. "Never underestimate the power of cuteness."

"And she should know," said Mistletoe sincerely.

The parakeet sighed. "Fine. But we still have two problems. First, how do we get Vinnie to wear a costume? He ran away from his owner because the man kept dressing him up."

Fuzzy squinted. "That *is* a problem."

"And what's second?" said Marta.

"How do we slip that costumed troublemaker out in front of the kids without getting him killed?" asked Luther.

Fuzzy scratched his jaw, opened his mouth to speak, then paused and thought again. Finally, he spread his paws.

"Tell me how you feel about this . . ."

CHAPTER 17

Reach for Disguise

Not long after that, the pets trooped back into their rat-occupied clubhouse with their arms full of disguises. Borrowed from dioramas, art projects, and pet costumes of previous years, their haul boasted a little bit of everything. Robots and rogues, superheroes and *Star Wars*, zombies and Zorros—a regular Halloween potpourri.

Vinnie looked up from where he lounged on a cushion munching a snack bar. "What's up with the fancy duds? Someone knock over a Halloween store?"

"It's costume time," cooed Cinnabun.

"Every year, when the students march in their

costume parade, we hold our own contest," said Mistletoe. "Last year, I was Cinderella!"

"Whoop-de-frickin'-doo," said the rat.

"As long as you're here, we'd like you to join us," said Fuzzy.

Vinnie waved him off. "Oh, no. I had enough playing dress-up to last me a lifetime."

The pets spread their costume pieces along one side of the clubhouse. With deliberate enthusiasm, they held up items, *ooh*ed and *aah*ed, and tried them on.

"Sure you don't want to join in?" asked Cinnabun, toying with a white helmet. "I think you'd look pretty handsome as a stormtrooper."

Vinnie scoffed. "Been there, done that."

"Nah, he's more of a werewolf," said Igor. He waggled the mask. "Check out the resemblance."

The rat cocked his head. "It *is* kind of a handsome devil. But nah."

Fiddling with a princess tiara, Cinnabun said, "Oh, and did I mention the prize for our contest?"

"Prize?" The rat's eyes brightened. But then he caught himself and plastered a cool expression on his face. "Some cheap plastic knick-knack, I bet."

"Why, hush your mouth," said the bunny. "It's nothing but the best here at Leo Gumpus. What's our prize this year, Sister Mistletoe?"

The mouse grinned. "Food. The winner gets a full-on banquet. Everything from celery and parsley—"

"Mmm, parsley." Fuzzy licked his chops.

"To slightly spoiled lunch meats and cheddar cheese."

The tip of Vinnie's tongue moistened his lips. "Cheese, huh?"

"And it's all good clean fun." Cinnabun batted her big brown eyes, pouring on the adorability.

Fuzzy fingered his Batman cape and mask. "You know, the students always dress me up as something silly . . ."

"Don't be so hard on yourself, Fuzzaroony," said Luther. "You were the noblest hamburger I've ever seen."

"So I take this chance to wear something that *I* want to wear." Fuzzy glanced over at the rat. "Mr. Herman must have put you in some pretty awful costumes."

"Ya got that right," said Vinnie.

"Wasn't there something *you* always wanted to be?"

The rat's eyes grew dreamy. "Ya know, matter of fact, there was."

"What was it?" asked Mistletoe.

"Batman," said the rat. "I always wanted to be the Caped Crusader, but never got the chance."

Clutching the cape and mask to his chest, Fuzzy said, "Er, Batman?"

"Yeah, I love those cartoons," said Vinnie. "Rich guy by day, mysterious crime fighter by night. And that Batmobile!"

"Nice ride," agreed Luther.

"Plus, ya gotta admit," said Vinnie, "the whole bat thing is wicked cool."

Cinnabun glared from Fuzzy to the bundle in his arms. Her meaning was clear: *Surrender the costume, ding-dong.* But Fuzzy wanted to be Batman himself.

He nibbled his lower lip, hesitating.

"I, uh . . . we just happen to have the outfit right here," he said at last, displaying the cape and mask.

"Sweet Gotham gooseberries!" breathed Vinnie.

With greatest reluctance, Fuzzy held out the costume to him. Vinnie slipped it on and struck a pose, paws on hips. "How do I look?"

"Positively dashing," said Cinnabun. Her glance encouraged the other pets.

"Handsome," said Marta.

Igor sniffed. "Very heroic, I'm sure."

The rat nodded, looking himself over. "Yeah, it suits me. I'm in."

"Great," said Fuzzy, trying not to resent giving up his costume.

Vinnie practiced a couple of Batman poses. "So when does this contest start?"

"Tomorrow," said Fuzzy, "right after school."

"All righty, y'all," said Cinnabun. "Meet here just as soon as your students leave the classroom tomorrow. We'll have ourselves a costume contest that's hotter than a billy goat in a pepper patch."

Their meeting over, the pets parted ways. As Fuzzy reached the top of the ramp, he glanced back. Vinnie had draped the mask over a pillow beside his makeshift bed, and was stroking the cape gently.

Fuzzy sighed. A shark wasn't nearly as cool as Batman, but it would have to do. Part One of his plan was in place: the rat had a costume.

He only hoped that Part Two would go half as smoothly.

If Fuzzy had thought his students were in the grip of Halloween fever, the next day, that fever reached its peak. All day long, the class bubbled like a shaken-up soda can. Almost everyone had worn their costumes, and Fuzzy was goggle-eyed at the variety.

Spiky Diego had turned up as a Wild Thing from *Where the Wild Things Are*, a book Miss Wills said fifth graders were never too old for. Heavy-Handed Jake's snow globe outfit was so bulky, he had to remove the globe part just to sit down. Maya had come as the Greek goddess Diana, complete with flowing robes and hunting bow, while Sofia looked positively eerie as a white-faced zombie bride.

Fuzzy shivered in delight.

Looking around the room, he spotted twin jellyfish (Natalia and Kaylee), a handful of Harry Potter characters, superheroes galore, and Ryan-with-the-glasses, clad in various pieces from caveman, pirate, vampire, and cowboy costumes.

Even Miss Wills dressed up as a Viking warrior, with a breastplate, golden braids, and horned helmet.

Needless to say, not a lot of schoolwork got done that day. There was some talk of math and social studies, but it kept getting sidetracked into Halloweeny topics.

Sometime after lunch, Miss Wills quieted the class. "Attention, everyone. I know we've talked a lot about the best costume for Fuzzy, and I want you to know I took everyone's suggestions into account."

"Does that mean he'll be Spider-Pig *and* a walking piece of sushi?" asked Loud Brandon. Several kids laughed.

"No," said the teacher, "but I'm afraid Fuzzy can't be a shark either, as I'd hoped."

"Awww," said a bunch of the boys.

"For some reason, the old costume pieces were hard to find this year," said Miss Wills. "Someone must have moved them." Fuzzy tried his best to look innocent. "So I had to improvise."

Strolling over to Fuzzy's habitat with a brown bag, the teacher continued, "I ended up combining two different suggestions into something new." From the sack, she withdrew a scrap of frilly pink fabric. Gently, she lifted Fuzzy into her arms and slid the cloth up over his back legs and around his waist.

"He's a ballerina!" squealed Sofia.

If guinea pigs could blush, Fuzzy would've turned twelve shades of red.

"Not quite," said Miss Wills, slipping a horned helmet just like hers onto Fuzzy's head. "He's Mighty Thor, Lord of the Dance!"

As the students clapped and cheered, Fuzzy twisted in the teacher's hands, trying to see himself. The helmet was pretty cool, but the tutu? How could Miss Wills put that on a self-respecting boar guinea pig?

Fuzzy's ears grew warm.

Suffering mange mites! All the other pets would laugh at him. But he couldn't ditch the costume for something he liked better, or the humans would know that Fuzzy was more capable than he seemed. He burrowed into the crook of Miss Wills's elbow to hide, and some of the kids went, "Awww."

Was it possible to melt from embarrassment? Fuzzy thought he might, but Miss Wills wouldn't allow it. Instead, she carried him up to her desk where all the students could admire him. And there Fuzzy stayed while the kids ate their treats, played their Halloween party games, and danced the Monster Mash.

Honestly.

It was enough to make a guinea pig wish he'd been born a moose.

CHAPTER 18

Giant Spiders in the Crawl Space

Is there anything longer than a school day when you've got something urgent to do afterward? Following what felt like the Mesozoic Era with some extra centuries tacked on for good measure, that particular school day finally drew to a close. The bell rang, and Miss Wills told the kids to line up in their costumes for the march over to the multipurpose room.

Hopping from one foot to the other with impatience, Fuzzy (a.k.a. Thor, Lord of the Dance) watched them go.

When the door closed behind the last kid in line, Fuzzy set a new personal record for scrambling out of his cage and up into the crawl space. Not even the tutu could slow him down. Charging along like a cheetah at a cat-food sale, he hurtled toward the clubhouse.

Timing was crucial. For their plans to work, Fuzzy and the rest of the pets had to reach the multipurpose room after the students' costume parade had started, but before it ended.

There was no room for error.

At last, Fuzzy reached the ramp. Without even slowing, he trotted down to join the others.

Boinga-boinga-boinga!

His rapid steps made the thin board wiggle like a hula dancer's hips.

He stumbled. He staggered.

Fuzzy tripped over his own feet, and—*bim-bam-ba-whump!*—tumbled head over heels to land in a heap at the foot of the ramp.

"Ta-daaahhh!" squawked Sassafras, spreading her wings wide to frame him. "I give him an eight-point-five for effort, but he didn't stick the landing!"

Igor clapped sarcastically as Fuzzy climbed to his feet, straightening his costume.

"Hurry, guys!" said Fuzzy. "There's no time to waste."

"To the Batmobile!" cried Vinnie. He looked all mysterious and superhero-y in his mask and cape—but not half as good as Fuzzy would have. "But first," said the rat, "an important question."

"Make it quick," said Fuzzy.

"Whattaya supposed to be, a warthog ballerina?"

The other pets choked with laughter.

Fuzzy flushed. "No, it's . . . complicated," he said. "No time to explain." Scanning the group, he noticed something. "Wait, where's Marta?"

All decked out in tiara and princess finery, Cinnabun waved him on. "She's meeting up with us in the crawl space—something about a tricky costume. Come on, let's shake a leg, y'all."

Luther shot her a meaningful look and then glanced down at his limbless body.

"Sorry, Brother Luther," said the bunny. "Um, let's shake a tail!"

One by one, the pets hurried forward to join them. Mistletoe wore a yellow-and-black bumblebee costume with antennae, and behind her came Igor, playing a scurvy pirate with eye patch and scarf. A witch's pointy hat perched on Sassafras's head, while Luther sported a stick-on goatee and a black beret tilted at a rakish angle.

"What are you?" Fuzzy asked the snake.

Luther smiled. "The coolest cat in town."

"Can't argue with that," said Fuzzy, leading the way back up the ramp. As the group entered the crawl space, Vinnie pulled up next to Fuzzy.

"Wouldn't it be easier to hold this costume contest in your clubhouse?" asked the rat.

"Oh, uh . . . tradition is important to us," said Fuzzy. "We always do this in the multipurpose room. It's . . . fancier."

"Huh," Vinnie grunted, falling back into line.

Fuzzy hoped the rat didn't question things too closely, or their plan might fall apart like a tissue paper tunic. He nervously gnawed on a whisker.

Much as Fuzzy tried to hurry everyone along, it wasn't the easiest task in the world. Sassafras's witch hat kept getting knocked off by struts and ducts. His own horns got stuck on first this obstacle, then that one. And Mistletoe's bee costume snagged on nails and splinters again and again.

When Fuzzy glanced back at them, the pets looked like the most ragtag band of trick-or-treaters ever to stroll a street. But still they pressed on. His heart swelled. Fuzzy admired their loyalty to a fellow pet, even if Vinnie wasn't one of their crew. Of course, he suspected Sassafras and Igor were only going along to see the kids' costumes.

At last, the pets had almost reached their first stop: the ceiling above a certain supply closet. Mistletoe had assured them that it was only a short run from there to the multipurpose room. Easy as catching a case of mange mites.

But when Fuzzy rounded a thick duct, a dark shape loomed out of the dimness. With its tangle of legs and great, globby body, it looked like a spider four times his size!

Wheek! Fuzzy shot into the air, bonking his helmet on a cross-strut.

"Oh, hello, dear," said Marta.

Clutching his chest, Fuzzy waited for the hammering of his heart to slow down to something approaching normal. A faint shaft of light revealed the truth. This was no mutant tarantula. Somehow, the tortoise had managed to attach eight hairy black spider legs to her shell.

"Nice, uh, costume," said Fuzzy.

"Ha!" Igor elbowed him in the ribs. "Little Miss Muffet here thought it was a real spider."

"S-so did I," said Mistletoe, her eyes white as fresh Ping-Pong balls in the dimness.

Trying to regain his cool, Fuzzy cleared his throat. "Okay, you all know the drill. We climb down through the supply closet. Then it's a short trip along the hall to the MPR's backstage door."

When he said that, the reality finally sank in. Fuzzy beamed. After years of longing for it, he couldn't believe they would finally get to watch the whole school march in the costume parade.

That was, assuming nothing went wrong.

Cinnabun surveyed the group. "Y'all keep a sharp eye out," she said. "Everybody should already be at the parade, but with humans, you just never know."

Igor and Fuzzy removed the ceiling tile, and one by one, the pets made their way down the jam-packed shelves to the supply closet floor. While several of them paused to readjust their costumes, Luther slithered up and turned the doorknob.

Carefully easing open the door, Fuzzy put his eye to the crack. Or tried to, anyway. *Clack!* His helmet bumped into the frame before he even got close.

"You shouldn't be—*heh*—*horn*ing in on our fun!" squawked Sassafras.

Cinnabun and Marta shushed her. "Now's not the time, dear," said the tortoise. "Adventure first, puns later."

The parakeet pouted. "Who says you can't do both at once?"

Doffing his helmet, Fuzzy checked out the corridor. "Nobody around. For safety's sake, let's go in pairs."

"Just like Noah's Ark!" piped Mistletoe.

"If Noah had a freak show on board," said Luther.

Fuzzy nodded to the snake. "Why don't you and Marta lead the way?" he said. "You can handle the back-stage door, right?"

Luther smirked. "Does a fat puppy hate fast cars*sss*?"

"Uh, yes?" said Fuzzy. The boa slithered out, with Spider-Marta trailing behind.

Fuzzy peeked through the crack. Not far off, a great hubbub of voices and spooky music echoed in the multi-purpose room. But no humans roamed the hallway. Down the corridor, Luther opened the stage door, and he and Marta disappeared inside.

Two by two, the rest of the pets followed, until only Fuzzy and Vinnie remained. Strapping his Viking helmet back onto his head, Fuzzy asked, "Ready?"

The rat eyed him. "Seems like a lotta trouble for one little costume contest."

Uh-oh, thought Fuzzy. *Of all the times for Vinnie to get suspicious* . . . "It's, uh, how we get our kicks," he said. "How much fun would it be if everything was too easy?"

The rat stroked his chin. Behind the black mask, his eyes were as hard to read as a kindergartener's Christmas card. "Beats me," he said at last. "I ain't never had it too easy. Come on, let's motor."

Heaving a silent sigh, Fuzzy led the way into the corridor. Practically vibrating with tension, he scanned left and right.

Their luck held; no humans in sight.

Just ahead, where the hallway made an L bend, stood the backstage door. Almost there! Fuzzy and Vinnie made for it at top speed, but just as they reached the corner, a pair of work boots clomped into view.

Fuzzy froze.

Above them loomed a sturdy figure in blue coveralls: Mrs. Drone. Her mouth gaped and her eyes lit with angry fire.

"*Rat!*" she cried.

CHAPTER 19

Chasers Gonna Chase

In that awful, frozen moment, the assistant janitor stood so close, Fuzzy could see right up her nostrils, flared like twin train tunnels of doom. Ignoring Fuzzy, Mrs. Drone glared at Vinnie. Her teeth clenched in a snarl.

"*Now* I've got you, you filthy rodent!" she growled, fumbling a pair of work gloves onto her hands.

A small part of Fuzzy took issue with her calling rodents "filthy." (Many were clean.) But a much bigger part of him was screaming the urgent message to . . .

"Run!"

In a flash, Fuzzy and Vinnie bolted for the stage door, Vinnie's cape streaming out behind like the real

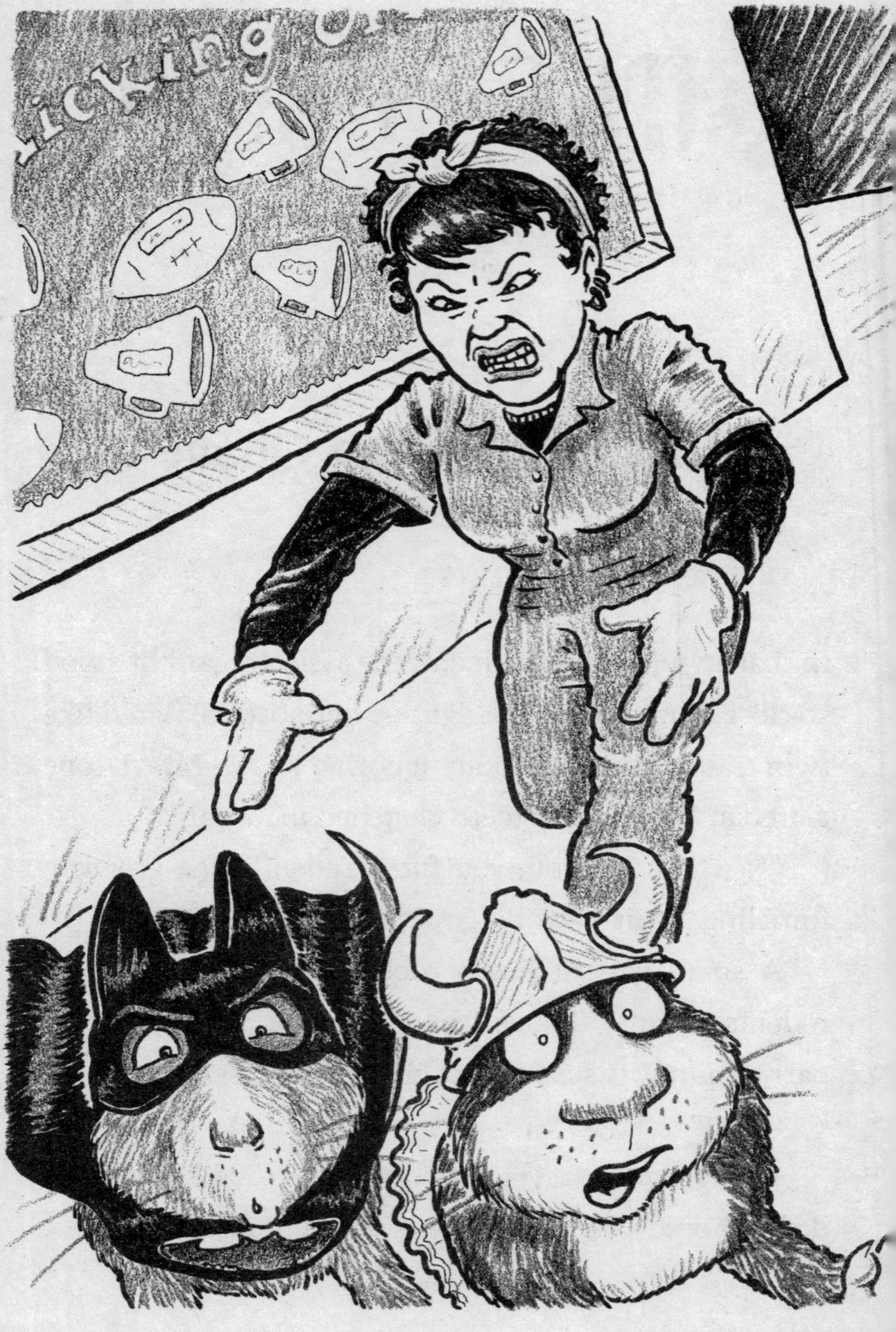
icking

Batman's. They galloped as if the devil were on their heels.

And she was. With a fearsome cry, Mrs. Drone dashed in pursuit. Her footsteps pounded down the hall behind them. As Fuzzy neared the door, he cried, "Luther! A little help?"

Luckily the snake was nearby. He sized up the situation in a second. When Fuzzy and Vinnie flew up the three short steps and past him, Luther arched his muscular body across the top stair like a rosy boa rainbow.

Not a moment too soon.

Up clomped Mrs. Drone behind them—until she tripped over Luther's coils and fell face-first with a *gonk!*

Fuzzy grimaced. That had to hurt.

While the assistant janitor sat up, dabbing at her bloody nose, Fuzzy, Vinnie, and the rest of the pets dove for cover. Luther slithered into a dark corner. When Mrs. Drone regained her feet, not a creature was in sight.

"You'll pay for that!" the woman snapped.

No answer from the pets.

"I know you're in here!" Mrs. Drone shouted over the thumping music and the chatter of voices from the other side of the red velvet curtains. "Don't think I won't find you."

Huddled behind a stack of folding chairs with Cinnabun and Sassafras, Fuzzy took a moment to catch his breath. Bluish lights illuminated the backstage, which smelled of paint and sawdust. A wild profusion of objects, from stage props to PE equipment, cluttered the shallow space.

"Looks like your plan to find Vinnie a home just went up in smoke," whispered Sassafras.

"A crying shame," said Cinnabun.

"Not necessarily," said Fuzzy. His gaze flicked from the curtain, to Vinnie, hiding behind a prop box, to Mrs. Drone. "If we can keep her away from him long enough . . ." Hurriedly, he whispered his plan to the other two.

"Pretty risky," said the parakeet.

"But it just might work," said Cinnabun. "Let's tell the others."

They slipped off in opposite directions, searching for the hidden pets. On the other side of the curtain, the crowd raised a loud cheer. Principal Flake's amplified voice boomed, "Let's hear it for the kindergarteners! Scary stuff indeed!"

Wiggling whiskers! Fuzzy was missing the costume parade.

His lower lip pushed out in a pout, but then, he felt embarrassed. Surely helping a fellow pet find a home ranked above having some Halloween fun?

Focus, Fuzzy, he told himself.

Poking his head around the stack of chairs, Fuzzy spotted Mrs. Drone creeping along in a crouch, arms stretched wide.

"Come to mama, you scabby varmint," she crooned.

Fuzzy couldn't help thinking that if Mrs. Drone were your mama, you'd be happier as an orphan.

The woman's gaze swept from side to side, seeking her target. "I'll put you out of your misery, Little Ratbag. *Crick-crack,* no more worries."

Fuzzy flinched. What kind of monster would do that to an innocent pet?

Well, maybe Vinnie wasn't all that innocent, but still.

Unknowingly, the assistant janitor was nearing Vinnie's hiding place. Fuzzy saw the rat tense, ready to bolt. And just then, Sassafras swooped out of the darkness, flapping her wings in Mrs. Drone's face and squawking up a storm.

"I'll get you, my pretty!" the parakeet cackled, getting into her witchy role.

"Ahh!" The woman shrieked, staggering back and swatting wildly.

While she was distracted, Fuzzy hissed, beckoning to Vinnie. "Over here!"

Quick as a hummingbird's blink, the rat darted out from his hiding place and joined Fuzzy behind the chairs. "Holy cheeseballs, what'd I ever do to her?" said Vinnie.

Fuzzy shook his head. "Nothing. She just really hates rats."

Sassafras flew off, and Mrs. Drone rooted around behind the box where the rat had been. But by then, Fuzzy and Vinnie had slipped away, crossing the stage and drawing nearer to the curtains.

Next, Mrs. Drone pounced on a basket of kickballs. "Aha!" she cried, flinging it aside. Up jumped Igor. "Arrrgh, matey!" he cried in his best piratical accent.

"*More* pets?" The assistant janitor reeled away, wailing, "Where are all these goldanged animals coming from?"

Taking advantage of the distraction, Fuzzy tugged Vinnie under a table. He hurried the rat along the wall, ever closer to the red curtains that bordered the stage. On the other side of the drapes, he heard the parade's joyful noise, and he scowled at the thought of missing it.

Across from Fuzzy, Marta, Luther, and Cinnabun were monkeying with a precariously balanced ladder. They were almost ready.

Now if only Mistletoe could pull off her part.

Resuming the hunt, Mrs. Drone snatched up a dust mop and began poking its shaft into hidden corners. Behind a trunk, under a costume rack, then beneath the low table where Fuzzy and Vinnie still crouched.

"Where . . . *are* you, you . . . evil, disgusting *rat?*" On the woman's last word, she jabbed the mop handle right between them, pinning Fuzzy's tutu to the wall.

Not daring to breathe, Fuzzy and Vinnie froze. Mrs. Drone bent down to check under the table, and just at that moment . . .

"Yahhh!" Mistletoe took a running jump off the tabletop, right into the woman's hair. With a screech, Mrs. Drone dropped her mop and staggered back.

"Jeezy peezy!" She batted at her curls.

But Mistletoe was too fast for her. The mouse scampered over the woman's scalp, dodging right and left, evading her hands. "Look at me!" she squeaked. "Bzzz, I'm a beeee!"

As Mrs. Drone stumbled backward, Fuzzy watched intently.

Just a couple more steps . . .

"*Now!*" he cried.

The pets tugged, the ladder swayed, and then, remorseless as a principal passing out detention, it toppled.

At the last moment, Mrs. Drone looked up.

Whang!

The ladder landed right on top of her, trapping her head between two rungs and bearing her downward. Nimbly, Mistletoe leaped off the woman's curls and onto the ladder.

Whoomp!

The assistant custodian hit the floor, and the mouse scampered off.

"Pull the cord!" cried Fuzzy to Igor and the others.

"What cord?" said the rat.

"Never mind. Let's go!"

Dragging Vinnie along with him, Fuzzy took shelter on the far side of the upright piano that dominated center stage. Here, they stood only a foot away from the curtains.

"Hey, we're running out of room," said Vinnie. "Don't wanna get cornered. Shouldn't we head for the back?"

Out front in the multipurpose room, someone had turned off the music. Fuzzy guessed they had heard the ladder crash backstage. He had only seconds to act.

"Do you trust me?" he asked the rat.

"No freakin' way," said Vinnie. "I hardly know ya."

From the corner of his eye, Fuzzy caught the other pets heaving with all their might on the cord that controlled the curtains.

It was zero hour.

"Do you want a nice home?" he asked Vinnie.

"Well, duh," said the rat. "Of course."

Fuzzy gripped Vinnie's paws in both of his. "Then act cute!"

Vinnie's "Huh?" turned into a "Huh*aaaaghh*!" as Fuzzy swung him around once, twice, and released him.

Just then, the red drapes parted.

Vinnie staggered into the gap, in full view of students and teachers. When he looked up and saw all those human faces staring his way, the rat froze like a woolly mammoth in a glacier.

In human talk, Sassafras squawked, "Look, everyone, it's Vinnie the Wonder Rat!"

CHAPTER 20

Pet Project

For an endless moment, nobody spoke. Fuzzy shrank back into the shadows between the piano's foot pedals, eyes riveted on the scene.

Alone at center stage stood Vinnie, paralyzed with shock. An ocean of costumed faces gaped—Wonder Women and witches, Spider-Men and skeletons—all staring at the rat. Then the voices started.

"Hey, look at that!"

"He's so *cute!*"

"Awwww!"

"What's her name? Minnie?"

"It's Rat-Man! *Nah-nuh-nah-nuh-nah-nuh-nah-nuh-nah,* Rat-Man!"

The kids surged forward to see, and Fuzzy marveled at the sight of them. Giant crayons, bananas, dragons, fairies, video-game characters, superheroes, cowgirls, Darth Vaders, kitties, and more. He was finally witnessing the costume parade, and his toes curled with excitement.

It . . . was . . . *awesome!*

Principal Flake stood just below the stage, dressed all in orange as the Great Pumpkin. Peering up at Vinnie, she said, "Someone's pet has gotten loose. Whose rat is this?"

Vinnie backed up several steps.

Fuzzy could see he was on the verge of bolting. *Hold still*, he thought. *Just a little longer.*

After checking around and seeing that nobody had claimed Vinnie, kids started shouting: "Mine!" "I'll take him!" and "He can come home with me!"

The rat glanced over his shoulder at Fuzzy, a confused smile spreading across his face. When Fuzzy looked into the wings, he saw all the other pets watching and grinning—even Igor.

"Here now, *someone* dressed him up," said Mrs. Flake. "I'm sure he belongs to somebody." But as it became clear the rat's owner was nowhere in the room, she began to waver.

Mrs. Sanchez, Room 4-B's teacher, stepped forward in her Zorro costume. "You know," she said, "when it seemed like we had a rat infestation last week, my students started asking why 4-B doesn't have a class pet. Maybe we could adopt him?"

"Yes, yes!" cried a group of kids, presumably her students.

"Well, um . . ." Mrs. Flake hesitated.

"*Pleeeease?*" the 4-B students chorused, making exaggerated begging gestures.

The principal surveyed the room again. "I guess if he really doesn't have an owner . . ."

And just then, something heavy collided with the piano, shoving Fuzzy forward. Recovering himself, he craned his neck to look around.

It was Mrs. Drone!

Dirty, dizzy, and disheveled, the assistant custodian stumbled onstage, leaning on the mop. She stabbed an accusing finger at Vinnie. "*You!* I've got you now!"

175

With a wild look in her eyes, the woman raised the dust mop like a batter hefting a Louisville Slugger.

"*No!*" burst from a hundred throats, including Mrs. Flake's. The principal held up her hands, but it was too late.

Fuzzy grimaced. He couldn't watch, but he couldn't look away.

Down swung the mop like the Hammer of Doom. At the last second, Vinnie dived out of its path.

Whack! The mop struck the stage so hard, its shaft splintered.

Off balance, Mrs. Drone fell to her knees. Her teeth were clenched in a snarl and her laser gaze still drilled into Vinnie. With nowhere to run, the rat leaped off the edge of the stage and into the principal's arms.

"There, there, little one," said Mrs. Flake, cuddling Vinnie. "You're safe now."

The assistant janitor gave a wordless growl, stretching out a pair of clawlike hands. "Give it to me. I'll rip the rotten little stinker limb from limb."

Turning half-away and shielding Vinnie, Principal Flake said, "You'll do nothing of the sort."

"I'll drown the sleazebag!" raved Mrs. Drone. "I'll poison it! I'll chop it up like broccoli!"

The principal's eyes narrowed. "This," she said, "is an innocent animal. And that is not how we treat animals in this school. Nor do we set poison for them."

"But you—" grunted Mrs. Drone, fingers twitching.

"Oh, yes," said Principal Flake, "I heard about that. And I never meant for you to go that far."

"But . . . but . . ."

Fuzzy edged back. The assistant janitor was practically foaming at the mouth, and he didn't want to catch her disease.

"It's tricked you, the filthy beast," moaned Mrs. Drone. "Give it to me. *Give it!*"

Mr. Darius pushed through the crowd and climbed onto the stage. Slipping his hands under his assistant's arms, he lifted Mrs. Drone to her feet. "Come on, Rhonda," he said. "Time to go home."

As the janitor turned, he happened to spot Fuzzy, still hiding between the piano's foot pedals.

Busted!

Fuzzy stiffened.

A curious look crossed Mr. Darius's face. For a long moment, they just gazed at each other, eyes locked. Fuzzy braced himself, waiting for the janitor to come scoop him up. Then Mr. Darius gave the tiniest wink and steered the woman off the stage.

Fuzzy blew out a long sigh. By the time he turned his attention back to the room, Principal Flake had handed Vinnie over to Mrs. Sanchez, and the kids of 4-B were cheering and crowding around to see him.

Fuzzy glanced at the principal. She hadn't noticed him, or any of the other pets who were peeping around the curtains to watch the proceedings. Fuzzy would've loved to stay and see who won the students' contest, but he'd pushed his luck far enough already.

When Cinnabun caught his eye, he nodded. Time for the pets to return to their cages before the kids went back to class.

The bunny gestured to the rest of the crew. Slowly, reluctantly, they turned away from the costume parade and faded back into the shadows like good little ghosts.

# CHAPTER 21

Let the Food Times Roll

Compared to all the fuss of the past weeks, the next day was relatively quiet. No one got brained with a ladder; nobody set a room on fire.

Of course, nobody turned up dressed as a giant human snow globe either.

Fuzzy found he missed that part.

In 5-B, the students finished their *Día de Los Muertos* unit by holding a brief ceremony around their *ofrendas*, sending good wishes to their ancestors. After that, they returned to their regular lessons—not without a few groans and protests. Class was back to normal.

Fuzzy didn't really know his guinea pig ancestors, but he sent up a good thought to all the class pets who had come before him. Like Fuzzy, they had sacrificed, sweated, and strived their best to bring happiness to their students.

Fuzzy only hoped he measured up to their memory.

After school, Fuzzy waited impatiently for Mr. Darius's visit. As far as he could tell, the man hadn't tattled on him after he'd spotted Fuzzy at the costume parade. No extra bars covered his cage. No new barriers stood in his way.

Fuzzy wondered why.

And then along came the janitor with his cart and broom, but without his rat-hating assistant. The man called a brief greeting, then began tidying up. Fuzzy cocked his head. Normally, Mr. Darius spent some quality time with him, shared a tasty treat.

Had Fuzzy done something to insult the man?

Then the cleanup was over and the custodian approached.

"Hey, little buddy," said Mr. Darius, slipping a slice of cucumber through the bars.

Fuzzy nibbled away, keeping his bright eyes trained

on the man. A treat was a good sign, but it didn't answer his question.

The janitor scratched a stubbly cheek. "You know, I saw you taking your little field trip yesterday."

Fuzzy stiffened.

Here it came. Farewell, freedom; hello, solitary confinement.

"But you know what I say? Live and let live," Mr. Darius continued after a long pause. "You want to have some adventures outside that little cage. I get it."

Relief flooded through Fuzzy. "Thanks, Mr. Darius," he chirped, though he knew the man couldn't understand him.

"I'm not going to bust you," said the janitor, stroking Fuzzy's back, "on two conditions. First, don't get caught, so I don't get in trouble. And second, be careful. You feel me?"

Twisting about, Fuzzy gave the man's hand some friendly licks.

Mr. Darius chuckled. "I'll take that as a yes. Oh, and you might want to avoid the cafeteria. My old assistant is working there now, peeling potatoes and scrubbing pots."

And with that, the janitor wheeled his cart out the door, wishing Fuzzy a friendly good night.

For a minute or two, Fuzzy just gaped. Humans were a mystery, all right. But Fuzzy knew one thing about them: Mr. Darius had to be the coolest human around (aside from Miss Wills, of course).

By the time Fuzzy joined the other pets in the clubhouse, the place was hopping. Literally. Someone had dragged a small music player into the room and turned up the tunes. Cinnabun was teaching Mistletoe and Sassafras how to dance the bunny hop while the others looked on.

Something smelled good, and Fuzzy noticed a school banner in one corner, draped over something lumpy.

"*There* ya are," said Vinnie, "the rodent of the hour!"

Fuzzy grinned. "How'd you like your first day as a class pet?"

"Sweet kids, nice digs." The rat kissed his fingertips. "And the chow is scrumptious. Mrs. Sanchez makes it herself."

"So she's different from your old owner?" said Fuzzy.

"Like a T. rex and a trike."

Fuzzy frowned. "I don't . . ."

"Different," said the rat. "*Good* different."

Drawing closer, Vinnie punched Fuzzy lightly on the shoulder. "Hey, kiddo, I just wanted to say . . . maybe I didn't always agree with yer methods, but ya did a good thing."

Fuzzy's ears grew warm. He ducked his head. "Aw, it was nothing."

"In fact," said Vinnie, "I'm gonna share my feast with you."

"Your feast?" said Fuzzy.

Vinnie glanced at the others. "Yeah. After all, I won the costume contest, didn't I?"

Finishing her dance lesson, Cinnabun turned the music down. "Well, actually . . ."

"Oh, come on," said the rat. "I was a wicked-cool Batman. Best costume in the building."

"Actually, you were Best Newcomer," said the bunny.

Vinnie cocked his head. "Come again?"

"And I was Best Traditional," said Sassafras. "Cinnabun was Cutest, Luther was Coolest, and Fuzzy—"

"Let me guess," said the rat. "Freakiest?"

Mistletoe raised a finger. "Most Creative," she said.

"So who won?" asked Vinnie.

Gesturing to the group, Cinnabun said, "Everybody."

"But . . . then, who gets the prize?"

Igor grinned. "Everybody!" He and Luther whisked away the banner in the corner, revealing a rich and varied feast spread along the clubhouse floor. Crunchy veggies, hearty grains, and aromatic cheese—a pet's delight!

A slow smile spread across Vinnie's face. "You guys are the weirdest bunch I ever came across. But ya know what?"

"What?" said Fuzzy.

"I think I'm gonna enjoy being a class pet."

Fuzzy patted his shoulder. "It's a pleasure to have you. Welcome aboard, Vinnie T. Rat."

And with that, all the pets sat down and began to feast, stuffing themselves good, like a class pet should.